DEAD MAN'S ODDS

Raider waited for a lull in the bar talk, then called in a loud, clear voice, "Kid! Danny!"

They whirled about simultaneously, each bringing his revolver out of its holster and thumbing the hammer back.

Raider's right hand dropped and lifted up his long-barrel Remington .44 with his finger tightly pressed down on the trigger. The heel of his left hand fanned back the hammer, which snapped back on the firing pin while Raider aimed the barrel at the Kid.

Each of the Pinkerton's shots had to hit home —there would be no time for second tries . . .

Other books in the RAIDER series by
J.D. HARDIN

RAIDER
SIXGUN CIRCUS
THE YUMA ROUNDUP
THE GUNS OF EL DORADO
THIRST FOR VENGEANCE
DEATH'S DEAL
VENGEANCE RIDE
THE CHEYENNE FRAUD
THE GULF PIRATES

RAIDER

TIMBER WAR

J.D. HARDIN

B

BERKLEY BOOKS, NEW YORK

TIMBER WAR

A Berkley Book/published by arrangement with
the author

PRINTING HISTORY
Berkley edition/April 1988

ISBN: 0-425-10757-4

A BERKLEY BOOK ® TM 757, 375
Berkley Books are published by The Berkley Publishing Group,
200 Madison Avenue, New York, NY 10016.
The name "BERKLEY" and the "B" logo
are trademarks belonging to Berkley Publishing Corporation.

PRINTED IN THE UNITED STATES OF AMERICA

10 9 8 7 6 5 4 3 2 1

CHAPTER ONE

The three horsemen picked their way through the gloom of the redwood forest.

"You ain't got nothing to worry about, kid," Denver Charlie said. "So long as we keep away from the path by the river, there's no way them sons of bitches can lay in wait for us here."

Ted Malloy nodded. Malloy was young, short, slight, pale from indoor work.

"You ever been up on a horse before?" Denver Charlie sneered at him. "You sure ride one like a bookkeeper."

"I *am* a bookkeeper," Malloy told him.

"I seen old ladies sit squarer in the saddle than you."

This made the third rider guffaw. This man's name was Gene. Like Denver Charlie, he was a heavily built man with some gray in his unshaven stubble. Charlie sported some long scars, but Gene had his whole left ear missing. Neither one was the sort of company an intense, nervous young man like Ted Malloy might be expected to keep. They didn't seem too comfortable with him, either. Gene said nothing, but Charlie poked fun at Malloy now and then to keep himself amused, alternating between taunting him and assuring him he would be all right.

Malloy needed assuring. This wasn't his job, taking the payroll in-country to the logging camp. He was only doing it while one of the two brothers who owned the logging company was away. He had been bullied into doing it by the remaining brother. Normally he sat at his office desk, handling accounts, giving cost estimates, tallying figures. He never handled money. The brothers did that. He earned a good wage for his work, and to a great extent he was his own boss, since the two brothers spent most of their time in the woods or loading ships. He didn't want to lose the job by refusing to take the men their pay at the logging camp. The lumberjacks could just as easily have collected their money at the town of Little River, where they would come in to spend it anyway, but they had always been paid inland at the camp and wanted no changes made now.

With all the troubles the Eagle Timber Company was having, they were losing men to other concerns every week. The fastest way to turn that drain into a torrent would be to make any change, good or bad, with the men's pay. So in one brother's absence, Ted Malloy had to take on the job of delivering the payroll to the logging camp. He could be trusted, and he could read, write, and count—very few of the Eagle Timber Company's employees had such dazzling credentials for the job.

Malloy wasn't just being disagreeable or lazy. He

didn't want to get shot. Carrying a payroll consisting of gold coins could cause a man's death faster than any disease in this part of California. Making it even more dangerous was the series of raids on the Eagle Timber Company. Some bunch of outlaws were hitting them harder than any other lumber concern in Mendocino County.

Denver Charlie was along for his protection. Charlie was a sure shot and a fast hand with a gun. It was said that he had killed some people in a misunderstanding over a faro game in Virginia City, back in Nevada, which was why he stayed put in the redwoods country although he wasn't a logger. He had been working for the two brothers for almost four years as a security man. Charlie had met Gene in a bar in Mendocino City and hired him as an extra gun.

The towering redwoods through which they rode on the way to the logging camp made the sunny day into twilight. Besides redwoods, nothing of any size grew on the forest floor to impede their way, though occasionally there were fallen giant trunks which they had to detour around. As Denver Charlie said, so long as they stayed off the beaten path along by the river, there was no way anyone could lie in ambush for them, because they wouldn't know which way they would come.

No one could sneak up on them easy either. The massive redwood trunks blocked the view in the forest after only a few yards. Rifles would be useless. Charlie carried a double-barrel shotgun. Gene relied on his Colt .45. Malloy was unarmed—he had told everyone he would hand over the gold without a fight if he was threatened. He had a weak chest, and he had come to California for his health, not to fight bandits.

"You're going to be all right, kid," Denver Charlie drawled. "We got less than an hour's ride from here."

The three men weaved their horses through the tree trunks at walking pace. The trunks rose straight and tapered to a roof of green tops high above their heads. The sunlight blinded them when they emerged from the forest into an open area that had been logged. As they crossed this open space, among the huge tree stumps— some bigger than a two-room cabin, a revolver shot sounded behind Malloy. He fell out of the saddle and lay unmoving, face down on the ground.

Denver Charlie, who was in the lead, twisted around in the saddle, scattergun held to his hip, ready to trip the hammers and loose off both barrels.

Gene slowly lifted his smoking .45 from its holster. "Dang thing went off by itself. Bullet grazed my boot."

Charlie kept the shotgun trained on him and snarled at Malloy, "Get up, you whoreson bookkeeper. If you don't move your ass out of this clearing real fast, you may get some hot lead up it. This treacherous bastard was sending a signal to his friends."

Malloy jumped up lively enough and headed for his horse at the edge of the clearing. The gold was in the saddlebags. If the horse bolted now and couldn't be found, he wouldn't have to worry about bandits, because Charlie would probably shoot him in a rage. He caught the horse and remounted it, even paler than usual.

Charlie hadn't taken his eyes or gun barrels off Gene, as the latter examined his gun and replaced it in its holster.

Gene explained, "I'll ride with the hammer on the

spent cartridge, so nothing can go off. Must've been a faulty shell."

Charlie nodded warily. "This time you ride ahead. Anything comes at me from the trees, I'll save one barrel for the small of your back."

"That wasn't no signal, Charlie," Gene protested. "I could have hit you easy with one bullet from where I was, and the kid don't have a gun. Why didn't I do that and take off with the gold myself?"

"You ride ahead, mister," Charlie told him, "and don't forget I'm right here behind you."

Gene took a long look at the shotgun barrels pointed his way, then did what he was told. Malloy hung back, riding almost alongside Charlie, hoping he was clear of the cone-shaped spray of lead that might come at any moment from Charlie's shotgun. They rode back into the twilight of the redwood forest, leaving the glare of the sun in the cleared area behind them.

A shot rang out. This time Denver Charlie pitched forward in the saddle and fell to the ground. As he fell, he loosed off one barrel of the shotgun. The muzzle was angled upward, so most of the shot missed its intended target, Gene.

Some of the pellets hit Gene's mount. The horse reared and plunged forward, unsaddling its rider.

Malloy took his chance while it was being offered. He dug his heels into his horse, shouted, "Giddyap!" and hung on to the reins and saddle horn as his horse cantered among the giant trunks. Malloy almost had each of his legs broken between the horse's side and tree trunks as the animal cut too close to the redwoods. He slowed the horse down.

No shots had been fired at him. He thought he heard

Gene calling him several times, but it might have been his imagination. If they caught up with him, he would drop the saddlebags and ride like hell. They would be sure to stop for the gold and maybe give him time to get away.

But no one caught up with him. He rode hard for more than two hours before he realized he had missed the logging camp and had no idea where he was.

Calvin Blair went straight from the railroad station to the headquarters of the Pinkerton National Detective Agency on Chicago's Fifth Avenue.

"I been on that train so long, it feels kind of peculiar to have solid ground under my feet again," he told Allan Pinkerton after he was shown into the founder's office.

"But the locomotive certainly beats a wagon train," Pinkerton said in his strong Scots accent.

"It surely does, sir. Me and my brother, when we was going out to California twelve years ago, didn't have no railroad across the continent, so we took a ship down to Nicaragua, crossed there where it's less than thirty miles wide, and then took another ship up to San Francisco. Looking out the train window at those dusty high plains on the way here, I'm sure glad we took that route instead of crossing by wagon train."

Pinkerton glanced at Blair's business card. "The Eagle Timber Company, Little River, Mendocino County, California. You and your brother partners?"

"Yes, sir."

"How do you get along?"

Cal Blair looked surprised by this question. "Why, just fine. We always have."

"Any other partners, past or present?"

"No, sir. Why do you ask?"

Pinkerton smiled at him grimly. "I assume ye're in trouble, that ye're not here on a social call."

Cal was a bit rattled by this big red-faced Scotsman. He had forgotten how brusque people could be back east. With them, it was state your business and be gone. "We're in trouble, all right. For more than six months we've been hounded by thugs who've burned our fixtures, smashed machinery, robbed us, and scared our workers away to other logging companies. We cut redwoods a few miles inland, haul them to the coast, mill them into boards, and ship them south on schooners to San Francisco, for the big building boom there."

"It shouldn't be hard for you to hire some guns to chase these thugs off," Pinkerton suggested.

"They're never the same ones who do it—or hardly ever. They just break up and disappear. That's what makes my brother, Abraham, think someone is behind all this, someone who is not just looking to rob or raise hell. He thinks that person hires different crews of drifters to harass us because he wants to take our company from us, now that it's making big money and has such good prospects."

"Have you any idea who this could be?"

Blair nodded. "Abe and I have narrowed it down to maybe a dozen suspects."

"That's not much help," Pinkerton observed.

"Well, sir, there's a rough class of men up in the redwoods. A lot of them ain't terribly particular about what they do to other people."

"So you want one of my operatives to find this man for you?"

"That's right, Mr. Pinkerton. I was thinking that

maybe if he came so no one knew he was working with us, he might find out more. And we need him to help out right away. There was a telegram waiting for me from my brother when I got to the station here in Chicago. Our main security man—a fella by the name of Denver Charlie—has been shot dead in a robbery attempt on our payroll. It seems a man named Gene he hired to go along with him was in cahoots with the robbers. But they didn't get the payroll. The bookkeeper carrying it ran off into the woods. It took my brother three days to find him—the poor young man was half dead from fright and hunger. We need your man to step in and take Denver Charlie's place. Charlie was large, fast, and mean, but that didn't save him. Maybe we need several of your operatives."

"I happen to have the kind of man you're looking for in Monterey at the present moment," Pinkerton said, checking a wall chart behind his desk. "His name is Raider. A very experienced man. But I must warn you —he's uncouth and prone to causing damage."

For the first time Calvin Blair smiled. "That's just fine, so long as he don't harm the redwoods."

For once in his life, Raider was glad to hear from headquarters in Chicago. His face burst into a big smile as he read the telegram. He was being reassigned from Monterey to someplace up the northern California coast called Little River. He had been in Monterey, a sleepy town south of San Francisco, for two months now, guarding the family members of a rich landowner. Their chorus of complaints about him to Chicago was nonstop: he used foul language, he spat, he drank, he showed no respect—their list was endless. Raider's only reply was that while he was in town, none of them got hurt. He sure hoped someone would kick their asses after he was gone.

He waited a day for the new operative to arrive, then took a train north to San Francisco. After the easygoing Spanish atmosphere of Monterey, San Francisco was a madhouse. The nonstop hammering drove Raider crazy. Everywhere he went, carpenters sawed planks and hammered nails. They were knocking houses together right next to one another, crowding them in between the bay water and the hills, then up the steep hill slopes. On every street, lumber was being unloaded off wagons. The carpenters swarmed like ants, nailing the boards together, so that a man could stand on a corner and watch the city grow before his eyes.

Raider had been in San Francisco a number of times before. Each time he came, he was always surprised at how much bigger the place seemed since he was last there. It was a simple fact that Raider didn't like cities. When folk crowded him in, he tended to push back. But of all cities, he found San Francisco most tolerable. The place was no longer as wild as it was said to have been in the gold rush days, thirty years ago, but it was none too tame either.

He headed back to the railroad station in time to meet Calvin Blair's train. The telegram from the Pinkerton head office described Blair as fair-haired and blue-eyed, "looking like a regular lumberjack." Although looking like a lumberjack no doubt had made him stand out in a Chicago crowd, it didn't do much to identify him among the train passengers at San Francisco, where most of the young men who didn't look like cowhands or miners or clerks looked like lumberjacks. Instead, Blair found Raider.

The six-foot-two Pinkerton was instantly recognizable to him with his black eyes, black mustaches, black Stetson, and battered old black leather jacket. A big six-gun hung on his right hip, against his sun-bleached denims. Blair introduced himself, and they shook hands.

Cal said, "Raider, back in Chicago they said the first thing you would want to do would be to find some whiskey and some women. You mind if we stop for a meal first?"

"So long as it don't take too long."

They both laughed at that, pleased with the fact they could get along with one another.

In the eating house, over a meat-and-potato stew, Cal said, "I half expected you to be some snooty Easterner in a derby hat, with a superior attitude to everything out here."

Raider smiled. "I used to work with a guy like that, but he quit so he could get married and settle down. I often wonder how he's doing."

They ate at a long wooden table with benches on either side. Crusts of bread and uncleared plates and mugs littered the long tabletop. Three other men ate farther down the table. Beyond them, at the end of the table, Raider noticed something move. A good-sized brown rat had jumped onto the table surface and was munching on a crust of bread.

The long-barrel Remington .44 revolver rose fast as a horse kick from Raider's holster. His right thumb snapped the hammer back, and his forefinger gently squeezed the trigger. The muzzle spat flame, and the bullet sped down over the tabletop, between the plates of the three men eating.

The rat squealed as the slug tore its body in two and splashed its blood on the dirty wall.

The three men looked up from their plates at the dead rat on one side and at Raider on the other. They went back to looking at their plates real fast, maybe for fear of causing him offense.

Cal Blair was impressed. "Raider, I think you're going to do just fine up in Little River."

Madame Lulu was Louisiana French, and she ran a cultured house, with no fighting or shouting allowed. Her girls were refined. Some could even play the piano or sing. They did not carry straight razors or derringers, and they did not rob their customers.

Raider refused the champagne Cal bought and purchased a bottle of real Kentucky bourbon. It had been a while since he had tasted anything other than rotgut, and a few glasses put him in a real mellow mood. He beckoned to a tall girl with big breasts and brown hair down to her bare shoulders to sit with him. Her silk dress rustled and her tits bounced as she walked over. Cal picked himself a sassy girl who hailed from New York and who never stopped talking.

Raider's girl said her name was Virginia because she was named after the state she was born in. Madame Lulu thought it was a pretty name for someone to have in her house, if none too accurate. She and Raider headed upstairs before he got too knocked out by the good liquor.

He threw off his clothes and sat naked on the side of the bed, pouring himself another glass of bourbon. Virginia disrobed modestly behind a screen, then scampered out naked and pranced around for him to admire her body. She came over and knelt on the carpet next to him. He brushed the hair from her eyes, and his fingers wandered over her shoulder and down her back.

Her sensitive fingers fondled his balls and stroked his erect cock.

His right hand eased down over her smooth, shapely back, tracing her firm flesh as her body narrowed into her waist and swelled out into her hips. He cupped one smooth cheek of her ass in his palm and softly squeezed it.

They embraced for a while and then slowly rose to their feet. He let his rigid member slip in between her thighs and felt her nestle it against her crotch.

Then they fell sideways onto the bed. She rolled on her back and parted her legs.

Raider drove the bulbous head of his cock between the outer lips of her sex and felt the smooth warmth inside. He drove his prong deep within her hungry body, and heard her gasp and sigh as he sent the full length of his manhood repeatedly into her.

She met his powerful strokes with a welcoming rhythm of her hips. She shouted and raked his back with her nails. He felt her body shudder beneath him, in a frenzied climax.

He brought her to four more savage, threshing climaxes before he released a stream of gism which he shot into her with a hot flame of pleasure.

CHAPTER TWO

Ted Malloy looked up from his accounts desk to rest his eyes from the columns of numbers. He worked in a small shack close to the sawmill. Apart from his desk, the shack contained only a four-drawer file cabinet, a shelf of books, a few chairs, a potbellied stove, and a pile of cut logs for fuel. He gazed out the window and idly watched a man walk alongside the mill toward his shack. His eyes suddenly focused, his body stiffened, and he squealed with fright. It was Gene. With one ear. Back to kill him!

He was about to run for the door to make his escape when he saw Abe Blair walking angrily toward Gene. Abe was shouting something that Malloy couldn't hear. Gene quickly sidestepped and picked up an ax that he spotted lying among some lumber. Holding the ax across his body, his left hand cradling the shaft just below the steel blade, he advanced on Abe Blair.

Malloy could see through the window that neither Gene nor Abe was wearing a gun. Gene knew that no one was allowed to carry a gun on the premises of the Eagle Timber Company, that he would not have been let in the gate with one. Ted Malloy's strong instinct was to hide or run, but in spite of his cowardice he was loyal to the brothers and liked them. Some weak spark of ferocity was struck deep inside him. Instead of running or hiding, he decided he would help Abe.

He reached behind the books on the shelf and drew out a Smith & Wesson Pocket .32.

"You pay me what you owe me or I'll split you from top to bottom," Gene growled at Abe Blair, twitching the ax blade so it flashed in the sunlight.

"You rotten son of a whore caused the murder of Denver Charlie, and now you have the gall to come to me and demand to be paid?" Abe laughed scornfully. "The bastard who hired you promised you could keep the payroll, didn't he? Share it among your friends. But since you were too stupid to lay your hands on the payroll, you ended up with nothing. Isn't that how it went? Look at all the trouble you went to, murdering a man and all, and you still ended up with nothing. Life just ain't fair."

"I had no part in that robbery," Gene claimed loudly. "I knew that little whippersnapper accountant would tell you I had. That's why I didn't come back here before this, along with being ashamed to have been able to do nothing to save Charlie's life. That runt of an accountant took off like a bat out of hell. He cared nothing about leaving Charlie and me behind."

"It was too late for Charlie, and Ted wouldn't be

seeing the light of day now if you'd caught up with him."

"I know it ain't no good to argue with you," Gene grumbled. "It's that runt's word against mine. That's all you got."

"I know," Abe conceded. "If I had a bit more evidence, the posse would have been after you. Consider yourself lucky I don't belong to some vigilance committee. If you hear about me joining one, you best move on real fast."

Gene showed him the ax head. "You join what you like. First, you pay me the wages you owe me."

"You'll get nothing from me."

Gene moved at him with the ax and gave it a trial swing at his head. Abe hardly bothered to move out of its way. The next swing was more serious, aimed at his chest. But Abe had no trouble in keeping out of the dead arc in which the ax blade traveled.

Abe Blair was smiling. He thought he had reason to be. Gene was no woodsman. He had never earned a single day's pay as a lumberjack. The way he swung the ax showed him up immediately. Abe realized that Gene was far more likely to hit his own legs or feet with his swings than he was Abe. Abe could see the justice in Gene hopping about on one foot for the rest of his life —though it might seem hard on a man to lose both an ear and a foot.

Abe made a short run at him, and Gene responded with a mighty swipe from right to left that buried the ax blade in the soil a few inches to one side of his own left foot. Abe was pleased. This vicious clown was going to mutilate himself—if Abe didn't get him first.

The big, heavily muscled man whipped the ax head

out of the soil without effort, ran a few steps forward, and took another gigantic swing. Abe had no difficulty avoiding the blade. He waited for Gene to follow through on his swing, moved in fast, and drove his right boot against the side of Gene's left knee. The big man's legs were slammed together and kicked out from under him. He fell heavily on his side, releasing his grip on the ax handle in order to break his fall.

Abe leapt on him like a wildcat. He snatched up the ax as he went, and, holding it in both hands, he pressed down the wood handle across Gene's throat while pinning his shoulders down with his knees. The harder Abe pressed down on the handle, the redder Gene's face grew and the louder his choking sounds. But he wouldn't quit struggling, and there was no way Abe was going to ease up until he did, even if it meant killing him.

It seemed suddenly to dawn on Gene that he was in danger of dying. With a massive burst of panicked strength, he threw Abe off him and rolled out of reach of Abe's chop with the ax. In an instant, both men were on their feet, but this time the ax was in Abe's hands. Unlike Gene, Abe was a skilled woodsman and could handle the ax like a surgeon could a scalpel.

He advanced slowly on Gene, who took some steps backward. Abe was beyond talk now. His blood was up. It was plain he meant to bury the ax head in Gene's bulk as he would into the sap of a redwood tree.

At this moment, the door of the shack flew open and Ted Malloy emerged, white-faced and wild-eyed, brandishing the six-shot pocket revolver.

He fired three times in rapid succession at Gene and paused, apparently expecting to see him fall to the ground. However, none of the three bullets came within ten feet of their intended target, although he was only thirty feet or so away. Malloy fired a fourth shot, and this time the bullet came close to striking Abe Blair.

"Quit shooting, you blind fool!" Abe yelled. "Leave him to me. I'm gonna make wood chips out of him with this ax!"

But Gene had used this diversion to put some distance between himself and Abe. He now suddenly charged Malloy.

"Fire! Fire!" Abe shouted to Malloy, chasing after Gene with the ax raised.

Malloy was confused and frightened. He held the revolver at arm's length in front of him in a shaking hand. He aimed, or tried to, at the big man bearing down on him. But he didn't squeeze the trigger.

Gene's big pair of hands clamped down around the chambers of the small gun, which would have prevented them from revolving—and the gun from firing—even if Malloy squeezed the trigger at this point, which he didn't. Gene wrenched the gun from the bookkeeper's hand and rounded on Abe, only seven or eight feet away—and the honed edge of the ax blade even nearer.

He fired twice and hit Abe twice in the center of his chest. Abe bit the dust. His dead face flopped to rest inches from Gene's boot.

Gene turned to the petrified Malloy with a smile on his face. He slowly and calmly raised the revolver so that its muzzle almost touched the trembling bookkeeper's forehead. Malloy stood paralyzed by fright.

Gene pulled the trigger, and the hammer fell on a spent shell. Its six shots were fired. The one-eared desperado cursed and tossed the gun to one side.

Men were pouring from the sawmill. They had heard the shots and now saw their boss stretched on the ground.

Gene grinned at the sweating bookkeeper. "Next time, kid," he said and headed for a gap in the fence around the company compound.

Raider and Cal Blair were down at the San Francisco docks at first light. Cal knew most of the crews on the schooners that transported timber. Most were Norwegian. Some schooners were returning north empty, after unloading their cargo of redwood planks in the city, and others were loading items needed by the logging camps and sawmill towns in the north—including twelve fancy women in French silks on one ship. None of the schooners were putting in at Little River, but three were bound for Mendocino City, only a few miles north of Little River, and their captains competed with one another in offering Cal Blair and his friend a free voyage north.

Cal indicated they would voyage on the vessel captained by a fair-haired giant with a beet-red face.

"Raider, meet Portwine Ellefsen," Cal said.

The smell on the captain's breath told that he had been living up to his name. The rest of the crew looked very hung over.

"They were singing a lot of sad songs last night about their loneliness for Norway," Portwine explained, as if that alone could account for their bleary eyes and shaky hands this morning.

The men set the sails on the schooner, and the craft caught the wind and moved away from the wharf. They sailed through the Golden Gate out into the Pacific, rounded Point Bonita and headed northwest to clear

Point Reyes. A fresh, variable breeze from the south kept the sails filled.

"If she keeps steady," the captain said, referring to the wind, "we could make Mendocino City by tomorrow morning. We'll be sailing close to shore, so you'll have something to look at today. I keep in close when I can, so I know what's going on in these parts. No point in taking another man's word for something when you can check it with your own eyes. There's a strong northward inshore current to help us along. It ain't as strong off California as it is off Oregon and Washington. Up there it takes whole redwood trunks as far north as Vancouver Island. The redwoods don't grow much past the California line. Them coastal Indians up around the Columbia and thereabouts ain't never seen three-hundred-foot-high trees or anything near that, so when these monster redwood trunks come floating up from the south, it gives them something to think about."

Past the mouth of the Russian River, Ellefsen had an insult, a joke, or a story about every mill or settlement they saw on the way north. The coastline consisted of cliffs from about twenty to a hundred and thirty feet high, with jagged teeth of rock jutting out of the sea at their base, over which the surf broke. Redwood, pine, and fir grew to the cliff edge everywhere. In some places, the redwoods and other trees had been cleared by woodcutters, and sheep grazed among the stumps.

The captain was skillful, steering his craft what seemed to Raider to be perilously near treacherous reefs and other vessels under sail. But Portwine Ellefsen knew his stuff, and he and his crew exchanged what sounded like cheerful insults in Norwegian with the men aboard other vessels they had challenged to a test of nerve and steering skill.

There were no proper harbors or inlets suitable for shipping, and timber was loaded aboard ships anchored in numerous small coves. These little coves, which provided no protection from waves and weather, were known as dogholes. The schooners usually would not come close to shore because of the rocks and shallows at the cliff base. The normal procedure was to erect one scaffold on the cliff top and another on some offshore rocks and suspend a chute between them with cables. The redwood boards, ties, and posts were slid down this greased chute, often two hundred feet or more. They were stopped short of the ship by a clapperman, who raised his trap to allow them to slide slowly onto the schooner deck.

At Saunders Landing there wasn't even a pretense of a cove. The chute ran from a ninety-foot cliff to a fifty-foot offshore rock and projected outward over the water, which Portwine said was five fathoms and where schooners could anchor safely. At Gualala, there was no chute. Cables were run from the sixty-foot cliff to the schooner's mast, and the loads of timber were run in bundles along it.

Ellefsen showed them the child's schoolroom atlas he had used to navigate with when he first arrived on this coast, twenty years previously. He claimed that although detailed charts were now available, he had more details in his head than could be put on any map.

The schooner moved farther away from land as darkness fell, for safety's sake. They passed the Point Arena lighthouse after midnight and changed from a northwesterly to a northerly course. The breezes kept strong from the south, filling the sails and driving the vessel quickly over the calm water. Even Raider, who had no liking for boats and deep water, was enjoying the trip. From what he had seen of the timber-loading operations along the coast during the day, he had developed a respect for the men involved in this dangerous work with ingenious ramshackle equipment.

They lay in Mendocino Bay until the sun rose. Then there was a further delay because the flag of the town's masthead was at half-mast, which meant that there was no room for more vessels at the anchorage. When a heavily loaded schooner left, the flag was raised and they came in.

Mendocino City was built along the northern shore of a half-moon-shaped bay on the mouth of the Big River. The collection of weathered, gabled wooden buildings was backed by hills covered in pine forest.

"You can see where the folks came from who built this town," Blair remarked. "They came from Down East, like my brother and me, good Maine men. That's why you have all them little New England gables. You see the steep pitch of those roofs? That's so deep snow don't lodge on them. Course you don't get snow in these parts, but that's how they build roofs in Maine, so that's how they built them here. You don't change a Down Easter's way of doing things all that easily."

They were in town only a short while when Cal heard of his brother's killing. He and Raider hired horses and rode south to Little River right away.

Raider and Cal Blair rode into Little River an hour before the funeral of his brother, Abraham. Cal loudly swore vengeance until the clergyman rebuked him, saying that was in the power of the Lord. Cal shut up, but the look on his face didn't change.

Everyone eyed Raider carefully at first. They were curious to see what Cal had brought back with him from Chicago, where they assumed he had come from. The brothers hadn't been able to keep it a secret that they were going for help to the Pinkertons. Things were worse off now than before Cal went. It was of more than passing interest to the workers whether this new man would be able to hold his own. Most of them were New Englanders or Canadians from New Brunswick, Nova Scotia, or Newfoundland. Many had come west to discover gold. All they discovered was that others had got there before them and left nothing behind. They fell back on the only kind of work they knew—lumbering. Apart from a little hardscrabble farming, logging camps and timber mills were the only sources of employment this far up the California coast.

Some of these Northeasterners had never seen anyone like the big Pinkerton before. They were used to woodsmen and occasional miners. They were hired and fired by frockcoated businessmen. But there were no plainsmen out this way, no bronco-busting cowpokers with leather chaps and jingling spurs. The workers would have made fun of Raider had it not been for the bad reputation these cow-town gunsels were making for themselves all over the West. And this dude with the black mustaches and black Stetson had a big revolver on his right hip that looked nicely broken in with loving care and frequent use. They decided to let him be for now. They knew they would not have to wait long to see what he was made of.

"How do I know you ain't in league with these robbers?" Raider snarled at Ted Malloy.

By now the bookkeeper's nerves were too far gone to withstand Raider in a belligerent mood. He had seen two men shot dead, and he himself had only missed meeting his Maker by a fluke of mathematics—he had fired off all but two rounds in the gun rather than three. Now for this criminal-looking Pinkerton to accuse him of betraying the Blair brothers and Denver Charlie was too much. He started sniffling.

"Don't you start wheezing like a sick calf at me," Raider shouted at him. "Cal, you got a jolt of anything to steady the kid?"

"I'll have some coffee," Ted said.

"The hell you will," Raider snorted. "I'll give you rotgut to loosen your tongue. But you ain't getting a damn thing else until I hear every bit of your story. You leave one little bit out, Malloy, and I get to hear of it after, I'll stomp you slowly into the dirt."

Ted Malloy told him everything that had happened, told him every detail he could remember, no matter how unimportant it seemed. He became less tense and spoke easier as the big Pinkerton listened patiently to him and nodded encouragement. When Ted had finished, he was surprised to find Raider's attitude to him completely turned about, no longer bullying and threatening.

"All right, Ted," the Pinkerton said, "you've had a rough time, so you lie low till you get over it. Anytime you see this Gene fella, you clear fast out of his way before he lays eyes on you. Find yourself a different place to work at the mill, so he can't find you easy. He don't know where you live. Better not hang out in the saloons for a while."

Ted looked shocked. "I never go into saloons."

"What else is there to do here?" Raider asked, assuming there must be something more lively than saloons in these parts.

"I belong to a discussion group. We meet three times weekly."

It was Raider's turn to look shocked.

Cal laughed and poured himself and Raider a drink from a bottle he had found. He said, "To Abe. May he rest easy."

"Amen," Ted intoned.

"I'll nail the bastard who done it," Raider growled and threw back the fiery liquor. "God, this is bad shit! You make this yourself, Cal? From redwood needles?"

Cal poured him another. "It's only the first one that tastes bad. After that, you can't taste nothing."

"Fucker didn't even bother to change his name," Raider muttered.

"Who?"

"Eugene 'One-Ear' Draper, that's who."

"You know him?" Malloy asked. "No one ever got to hear his last name, but that's not so unusual in the redwoods country. You sure it's the same man?"

Raider shrugged. "The way you described his ear cut off close to his head. A Comanche done that to him, so I've been told. And he calls himself Gene. I like his old name better. One-Ear. How many fellas do you think are west of the Mississippi who answer to that description? Who knows? Maybe there's a few. But we don't have to worry about that, because if this is the same son of a bitch I call One-Ear, I'll know him from my own personal past experience." Raider spat on the floor to emphasize his point.

* * *

Little River, on the mouth of the river of that name, was smaller than Mendocino City but just as busy. Besides two timber mills, several shipyards built schooners there. The ships were built at the edge of the water, without any of the docks and cranes that a shipyard back east would possess. Raider looked the place over, impressed as he had been the previous day on shipboard by the way folks got things done out here.

Having got an idea of the layout of the place, he headed for the saloons and found the Skid Row to his fancy. The saloon was named after the path cut through the forest to haul out redwood logs with teams of oxen. The customers were all lumbermen, shipbuilders, or ship's crewmen, and a silence fell on the place when Raider walked in and they all looked at him.

Most men in Raider's place would have decided that this was a less than friendly welcome, but Raider never bothered himself with trivialities like that. He liked the place because it had no chandeliers, no beveled-edge mirrors, no piano—none of the geegaws that, in his opinion, were rapidly spoiling places where a man used to be able to come in to have a few drinks and relax and not worry about breaking something valuable in a careless moment.

The whiskey he was served was the same rotgut Cal had given him at the mill. But Cal had been right—after the first one, the others went down easier.

A man bellying up to the bar said in a taunting voice to Raider, "Did you bring your herd out this way, cowboy, and lose a few steers in the redwoods?"

That got a lot of guffaws along the bar, followed by a moment of quiet to hear what Raider had to say.

"Naw, I'm looking for a fella name of One-Ear Draper. I hear he's been calling himself Gene. You know him?"

"I seen him once or twice in Mendocino City," the man said, "but not in Little River. Too bad what he done to Abe Blair. Abe wasn't a bad fella. You think you're gonna be able to handle this One-Ear?"

"That's what I get paid to do," Raider said shortly.

The man looked at Raider cautiously and decided to say nothing more. Another man along the bar took up where he left off.

"Me, I don't give a rat's ass for this Gene One-Ear. I seen him, and he's not one of us—he don't work lumber. He ain't one of us, and you ain't one of us, so what do we care? Just so long as you don't get in the way of us loggers. Do that and you're in trouble, stranger. You understand me?"

Raider looked this man over. He had shoulders and arms that appeared capable of tearing up trees by their roots. The Pinkerton smiled. "I came here to protect you boys from him."

That stung the logger. "*You* protect *me?* That's a laugh. I'm gonna finish this drink, cowboy, and if you're still at this bar when I come walking along, duck your head as I pass by, cause my fist is gonna be aimed at your head."

He wasn't wearing a gun, and Raider reckoned he had no right to go for his own gun unless the logger drew the big knife in a sheath on his belt. This was the kind of confrontation Raider liked least. Men like this logger kept their muscles supple by fistfighting when they weren't working. The trouble with fistfights, so far as Raider was concerned, was that even the winner took a beating. In his line of work, a man had to try to avoid getting hammered too often—it loosened the brain.

Sure enough, in a few minutes Raider saw the lumberjack come along the bar toward him. The nearer he got, the bigger he looked. One blow from either of those sledgehammer fists would stun an ox.

Raider said, cold and casual, "Why don't you go home and get your gun? I'll wait for you here."

That took maybe half an ounce of confidence out of the woodsman. He looked at Raider uncertainly for an instant, then looked away and kept coming. The Pinkerton waited—until the man was level with him and ready to deliver his blow. Raider grabbed the neck of the nearby full whiskey bottle on the counter before him and struck a hard downward blow at the man's face.

The lumberjack's fist shot out in a hard straight right to Raider's head, but Raider kept back out of reach. The added eight or nine inches of reach the bottle gave his arm allowed him to score a blow and remain untouched himself. The thick glass at the base of the bottle crashed down on the bridge of the lumberjack's nose, crushing the cartilage and flesh.

The man howled with pain and swung his fists wildly about him, decking one man who went to help him. He was blinded by tears of pain and half choked on the copious flow of blood. He staggered out the door into the street, cursing and gasping for air.

Raider replaced the unbroken whiskey bottle in front of him on the bar.

The bartender eyed the level of the amber liquid in the uncorked bottle. He said in an unfriendly tone, "You have to pay for what you spilled."

CHAPTER THREE

Eugene "One-Ear" Draper sat in a dark grove of giant redwoods outside Noyo, a doghole north of Mendocino City and Little River. He rolled a cigarette and lit it from the butt of the one just smoked. Stanton was late. That meant he wasn't pleased. One-Ear thought he should be. But there was no pleasing some people.

When Stanton finally showed, he dismounted and took his time about tying his horse at a patch of grass in a break in the trees. Stanton was short, no more than five-two, lean as a whippet, sharp-featured, fast-moving, and fast-thinking. One-Ear hated his guts. But Stanton paid well, even if he was never satisfied.

"Why did you do it, One-Ear?" Stanton asked, not looking him directly in the eyes and speaking slowly, loudly, and distinctly, like he was talking to a child or a deaf old man. For some reason, Stanton always talked to him like that, although he talked quite normally to other people.

"Do what?" One-Ear asked.

"Kill Abe Blair."

"He come after me. I was down in the mill compound to snuff out that little bookkeeper who's been badmouthing me. He's the only witness. I thought once he was gone, there'd be no one to point a finger at me. Abe Blair come at me like a madman. It was the bookkeeper who had the gun, not me. Blair was after me with an ax. I had to shoot him."

"Certain people ain't too happy about what you did," Stanton said, his gray eyes flinty above his sharp nose.

"That beats the hell out of me," One-Ear said. "I thought they'd be hootin' and hollerin' with happiness at what I did. Ain't that what they want? Don't they want them Blair bastards bankrupt and dead?"

"I guess so, in the end. But in the meantime, they want to be the ones calling the shots, not you. They got plans and concerns that you and me know nothing about. When you go off like that on your own, there's no telling how you could mess up what they have arranged. They have everything set out in a line. They want things to happen in a certain order, the way they say."

"Pity they themselves didn't have to face Abe Blair with an ax in his hands," One-Ear grumbled. "They might have been pleased to go along with a quick change of plans then."

"They don't have to face anybody, because they pay me and I pay you. So long as they pay good, they get what they want."

"All right by me," One-Ear agreed. "I only wish I

knew who these godalmighty folks are. I could tell them a thing or two."

"You won't ever know who they are if you stay lucky, One-Ear. Soon as you start getting any ideas who they might be, they won't have no more use for you."

One-Ear sulked. In reality, he had no idea who was giving orders, but he felt there was no harm in letting Stanton think he might have some idea. It wasn't Stanton himself who gave orders. He was only a middleman, with no land, money, or backing of his own. Stanton could act high and mighty, but One-Ear Draper wasn't fooled. Stanton was just a hired hand, same as Draper. He might be faster-thinking, but if it came to a showdown between the two of them, Stanton's brains wouldn't be enough to save him—One-Ear was sure of that. He would come out on top.

"I still say I should get a big bonus for nailing Abe Blair," One-Ear said truculently.

"You're lucky to get anything at all," Stanton told him. "You were told you could keep the payroll, but you lost that. No one told you to kill Abe at this time. Forget your bonus."

One-Ear glowered but said nothing.

Stanton felt relieved. Draper wasn't happy, but he was going to accept what Stanton said. The truth was, of course, that his boss had been delighted at Abe Blair's death and had paid a thousand dollars in gold as a bonus for it. If Stanton did not have to pass it on to Draper, he would be a thousand dollars richer.

"You didn't get the payroll when you were supposed to, and you killed one of the brothers when no one asked you to," Stanton went on. "You think that's going to make the people who pay us happy? But you want to make some money, right, One-Ear? Some real money. I got someone for you to kill. You do the job right and I'll see to it you get a big payment."

Draper grinned. "Who do you want me to kill?"

"This new fella they have at the timber mill, the one who took Denver Charlie's place. He'll be riding with the payroll this week. You blast him and keep that payroll. I'll have his time of departure and route beforehand for you."

"What's this fella like?"

"I dunno. I heard his name, but I forget it," Stanton said. "It don't mean nothing. He's one of them yella-bellied Pinkertons."

"I don't want nothing to do with Pinkertons," Draper said hoarsely.

Stanton looked at him carefully. "You losing your nerve?"

"No, I ain't."

"You spend your time bitching, One-Ear, after you fuck everything up. Then I ask you to do a simple thing for good money and you start getting nervous. Hey, this fella isn't the whole Texas Rangers. He's one lousy Pinkerton. What's wrong?"

"I been unlucky with Pinkertons," One-Ear said grimly.

"So change your luck. It don't pay to be superstitious. Can I depend on you?"

One-Ear nodded. "I guess so. I need that payroll."

"I was born and reared in Arkansas," Raider told Midnight Olsen, captain of a rival schooner to Portwine Ellefsen's. "I never saw the sea until I was twenty-five."

"Where is Arkansas? In the middle somewhere? *Ja,* I

was born a stone's throw from the sea, and I get uneasy when I don't hear the waves in the background. In the woods, it is very silent. I hurry back to the coastline."

They were sitting at a table in the Skid Row saloon in Little River, looking out the open doorway at a spectacular sunset over the Pacific.

"All that water sloshing about and banging against rocks all the time makes me feel like I might enjoy a quiet spell on the prairie," Raider said. "I don't trust all that water."

"No seagoing man ever does," Midnight said. "A man who isn't afraid of the sea goes out on it when he shouldn't and gets hisself drownded. All of us is afraid of the sea and very careful, so we don't get drownded as often."

"But you do?"

"Oh, sure," Olsen said. "Every big storm, two or three ships are lost along this coast."

"Coming up with Portwine Ellefsen, I was wondering if I could swim as far as the shore if the ship went down. I dunno if I could have made it."

Olsen looked at Raider in surprise. "You can swim? I can't swim a stroke. Most seafarers here don't swim. *Ja*, we figure it will be a quicker death that way. Even if you made it to shore, you would be broken against sharp rocks by the waves."

Raider swallowed his drink. "That's all I need to hear. Hell, when this is done, I think I'll walk south to San Francisco."

"There's no trail. You can't take a horse. But you don't worry, Raider. With the likes of Ellefsen and me, you couldn't be safer. Watch out for the young men, though. They think they know everything. That's what happened to the *Electra* a few days ago."

"She went down."

"*Ja.*"

"But there was no storm," Raider said.

"A foolish sailor doesn't need a storm. You notice the spring tides we had. The captain from Fort Bragg lost his bearings and thought he was at another place because the high water covered up some landmarks. The ship hit a reef which normally you can see. The rocks tore the bottom out of her. Seven men saved, four lost. On a calm, sunny day."

"I been wondering about those big tides. They say the moon controls them. How come some are bigger than others?"

Midnight Olsen poured them each a generous measure from his bottle and rubbed his hands in anticipation. This was the kind of talk he enjoyed—about the sea. "Everyone knows about moon-pulled tides," he said, tugging at his huge black beard. "What they don't know about is the sun-pulled ones. They are only maybe one-third as high, but they take place twice every twenty-four hours, just like the others. You get your spring tides—and spring ebbs, too—when the solar and lunar tides both come more or less together; that is, when the earth, moon, and sun are all in a line with one another."

"When's that?"

"At full moon and new moon. Twice a month. At full moon, the earth is more or less between the sun and the moon, so we can see the whole lit-up side of the moon. At new moon, the moon is between the earth and the sun and we can only see a small part of the side being lit by the sun." He went on to say a lot more, some of which Raider understood.

Raider was finally lost somewhere in celestial navigation, and he said good night. "I have to make an early start tomorrow. I'm taking the payroll in to the logging camp."

Olsen gestured at him to keep his voice down, for they were in earshot of a lot of men at the bar.

Raider laughed and said, "I reckon there's no one in these parts with the balls to try to take that payroll off me."

Midnight Olsen shook his head in disapproval. This was the kind of talk that sank ships.

Ted Malloy finished counting the gold, went over the pay list with Raider one last time, and put everything in the pair of leather saddlebags. "I won't be riding with you, Raider, and I don't care who knows the reason— I'm scared shitless!"

Raider punched him playfully in the chest. "But you're honest, Malloy, and I'll settle for that anytime. Don't think too badly of yourself. When the chips were down, you came out with a gun to help Abe Blair."

Malloy's face fell. "We all know the results of that."

"Sorry, I didn't mean to bring that up," Raider said. "I been responsible or half responsible for so many deaths, I ain't too sensitive on the subject. Look, Malloy, you done your best, and you're still trying."

Raider was being very friendly to him because he was so pleased at the news that Ted Malloy wasn't coming with him. Up until yesterday, Malloy had been insisting on coming along. The last kind of person Raider wanted along with him was someone who might crack under the strain. People with high principles were fine in drawing rooms, according to Raider, but they did less well out in the murderous reality of a Pinkerton's world. Raider picked two men to go along with him, Bill Theyard and Silas Hanks, both friends of Denver Charlie, both men with a simple wish to get back at his killer. That was the sort of thing Raider knew very well; he knew he could handle them and that their rage was deep enough to make them dependable.

Cal Blair wasn't saying much. He was letting Raider run his own show at the sawmill, hanging back, appreciating how the big Pinkerton got his message across. Raider was being plain and straightforward with the men. Any man who took sides against the Eagle Timber Company was picking a personal quarrel with him. Any man who wanted a showdown could have one. Any man who wanted to say something in a private talk could trust him. Any man who wanted to mess with him would be buried at company expense.

The three men rode away from the mill on the coast, into the dark forest.

"Those dumb sons of bitches will be expecting it to happen the same way it did last time," One-Ear Draper told the three men with him. "They won't believe we'd come in this close to the mill. This way we'll get them before they lose us in the trees."

The four of them sat on their horses just out of sight of the sawmill in a dense stand of pines. Draper had taken on the three men the previous day in a Noyo saloon, and they had spent all night here in the woods waiting. The agreement was to split the payroll in six shares, with One-Ear taking three of them—one each for being finder, leader, and team member. He bought them food and booze in Noyo before they left. Since they hadn't eaten in two days, they were agreeable to what One-Ear wanted. He promised them easy money, and they were ready to listen to that kind of talk.

In a while, they heard horsemen approaching. The four men pulled bandannas up over their faces, and Draper pulled his hat down sideways to cover his missing ear. At a nod from One-Ear, the men cocked the hammers of their double-barreled shotguns.

"I don't want no mistakes this time," Draper whispered. "Ride right up to them fast. If any of them make a move, blast them."

They waited a while longer, until the moving shapes of horsemen could be seen flitting between the tree trunks. Draper spurred his horse forward, and the others followed close behind him. All four got very close before they were noticed, and by then it was too late for their victims to run or hide. The bandits quickly surrounded the two riders, who drew their six-guns but dared not use them against the superior firepower of four double-barreled shotguns.

"We don't want no trouble," Draper told them. "You put them guns back in their holsters and you won't come to no harm. You hang on to them and I'll blow you out of the saddle." He waited for both men to holster their guns, which they did in a hurry. Then Draper dismounted and detached the pair of heavy saddlebags from one man's horse. "You the Pinkerton?" he asked.

"Huh? I ain't a Pinkerton."

Draper stood there, the saddlebags suspended from his left arm, looking up at the two horsemen. He swiveled around his shotgun toward the second man. "Then you gotta be the Pinkerton."

"No, I ain't," the man said. "Neither one of us is a Pinkerton."

"Look, I aim to kill whichever one of you is a Pinkerton," One-Ear said, getting annoyed by the delay. "The other man can go. So he better point out the Pinkerton to me, so I don't have to kill you both, which I will if I don't discover which of you is lying to me."

"We ain't lying."

"Neither one of us works for the Pinkertons."

"One of you's gotta be!" Draper yelled.

"I'm the Pinkerton," a voice said from behind them all.

The three bandits still on horseback twisted in their saddles to face this intruder, swinging their shotgun barrels around. He was on foot, a tall man in a black Stetson and old black leather jacket, who held a long-barreled revolver in his right hand.

The Remington .44's hammer snapped down on a cartridge cap, igniting the charge inside the brass case and forcing the lead bullet out of the barrel on a surge of explosively expanding gas. The mounted bandit in the middle caught the slug just below his left armpit. He could only manage a stifled gasp as the bullet turned end over end in his body cavity, tearing through his left lung and then his heart muscle.

While this man was still leaving the saddle, Raider flipped back the hammer and brought it down again. From the front, it was a clean shot that left a dime-sized hole in the middle of another bandit's forehead. From the back, it was a messy job, because the bullet tore out a fist-sized chunk from the back of the skull and spread the bandit's brains some distance around.

The third mounted bandit almost got off a shot from his scattergun. It was that close. But in that last fraction of a second, the man knew he was too late, that he was going to die. The Pinkerton was too fast for him—his aim was too deadly accurate. Before the bandit could get the barrels leveled on his aggressor, before his finger could haul back on the trigger, the big Remington .44 spoke a third time. A long tongue of flame sprang from its muzzle, and the lead projective found its mark, shattering a rib bone as it entered the man's chest.

Raider pulled down the bandannas and checked the faces and ears of the men he had shot. The fourth man had to be One-Ear. The two lumberjacks pointed: he had taken off into the trees. The Pinkerton went after him on foot in the direction they pointed, while the two men searched on either side of him on horseback. Raider soon heard a shot and one of the men shouting, "This way! Over here!"

One-Ear Draper had not gotten very far, weighed down by the heavy saddlebags he had slung over one shoulder. He had fired the shot at the horseman pursuing him. He had missed, and now he fired again and missed once more.

"Leave him to me," Raider ordered in a loud voice. "This is kinda personal between him and me. You hear me, One-Ear?"

There was no reply from Draper, who was still trying to get away among the trees. By now his bandanna had slipped off his face and his hat no longer covered his mutilated ear. Raider chased after him until he was hailing distance once again.

"You want to stop and face me down, One-Ear? Or you wanna quit? If you keep running, I'll put a bullet in your leg. One of these .44s can make splinters of a leg bone."

Raider waited a moment, then stopped and took aim at the figure twisting among the tree trunks. His forefinger pressed down softly on the trigger, and the revolver kicked in his right hand.

Draper felt the bullet brush his leg as it went past. It drew no blood and broke no skin, just nicked the denim of his pants. One-Ear knew this was no fancy shooting. The Pinkerton had been trying to make dust of his thighbone, so he'd never walk straight in his life again. He had recognized Raider the moment the Pinkerton had surprised him and his men in the act of robbing the payroll. He remembered Raider real good, and figured nothing would please the Pinkerton so much as making him a cripple for life. The heavy saddlebags were weighing him down, but he wasn't going to leave all that gold behind. There was nothing to do now but to turn around and fight. . . .

The two men closed the distance between them until it was less than twenty yards. Each had a revolver in his right hand—One-Ear having thrown aside his shotgun when escaping the scene—and there was nothing to keep them from shooting at any moment. All the same, neither man opened fire.

"I thought I'd never lay eyes on you again, One-Ear. Not after you broke out of custody back in Montana."

Draper's face cracked open in a snarling grin. "When I heard there was a Pinkerton assigned to the timber company, it crossed my mind it might be you. But I figured there was only a small chance of that."

"You guessed wrong."

"I sure did. Nothing about this thing has gone right for me from the start. But I got the payroll in my hand right now"—he lifted the bags suspended from his left hand—"and I ain't giving them back to you. I reckon that means we got a fight on our hands, unless you got sense enough to back down this once and let me get away."

"You ain't got nothing worth fighting over," Raider told him.

"I'll fight you for this gold," One-Ear growled. "Best man wins."

"Maybe you should count that gold first, before you decide to die for it," Raider said. "Look at me. I'm going to holster this gun to give you a chance to open them saddlebags."

Draper watched him, surprised at the Pinkerton's action, wondering whether to take advantage of this momentary edge he had over his opponent or whether to satisfy his curiosity about the gold in the saddlebags. The gold won out, and One-Ear pushed his Colt .45 into its leather holster. He set about opening one of the saddlebags while keeping his eyes on Raider, ready for any low-down tricks he might play.

He wasn't ready for the one Raider had already played on him. The saddlebag he opened was filled with stones from the ocean beach.

Raider slowly drew his six-gun and walked in measured paces toward him. One-Ear was cursing up a storm and kicking the saddlebags, which of course hurt his feet because they were filled with stones, which naturally made him curse louder.

One-Ear moaned, "I could have got away if I hadn't been dragging this load with me."

He was willing to fight to the death for gold. These bags of stones so took the heart out of him, he put up no fight and let Raider take his gun and bind his wrists behind his back with a length of rawhide thong.

The genuine payroll was in the saddlebags on Raider's horse, tied a ways off in the forest. After they mounted One-Ear Draper back on his own horse and tied the three dead men across their mounts, they tied all four horses in a line on a lariat and secured its loose end to Silas's saddle.

"There'll be a riot out at the logging camp if the payroll is late," Raider said to him. "Me and Bill will ride out with it while you take Draper back to the sawmill. Now, I know this bastard killed your buddy Denver Charlie, and I know you hate his guts, but that don't mean he won't arrive alive and well at the sawmill. You understand what I mean? This ain't your turkey. He's in Pinkerton custody. If he happens to get shot accidentally on purpose, or anything else, you're gonna have to deal with me."

Silas nodded and began his short ride back to the sawmill through the trees, trailing behind him first Draper and then the three dead bandits tied belly down across their saddles.

"Makes a real pretty picture, don't it?" Raider said to Bill before they turned into the interior in the direction of the logging camp.

Silas Hanks hailed from Passadumkeag, Maine, and he took the Pinkerton's words very seriously. Every couple of minutes he would look back sharply over his shoulder to make sure his prisoner was behaving himself and that none of the dead ones had come back to life. It was slow going among the trees, since the horses were unused to being led on a line and often tried to walk abreast or around different sides of a tree. Silas took out his anger on the horses and said nothing to One-Ear, who was carefully behaving himself.

After one strong outburst at the horse that left Silas red-faced and dissatisfied, One-Ear said, "I sure could use a toke of brandy from that flask in my bedroll, if you was agreeable, friend."

Silas's eyes lit up. "Brandy, you say? How do I know you ain't trying to poison me?"

"Give me the first few swallows. If I don't roll over dead, I guess it'll be safe for you to take a sip."

Without dismounting, Silas rummaged in the bedroll tied behind Draper's saddle, saying, "Don't go getting no notions I'm going to get drunk and let you get away."

"There ain't enough there to get either one of us drunk."

The flask was solid silver and small—holding only half a pint. Silas uncorked it, sniffed suspiciously, and held it to Draper's mouth. One-Ear swallowed a mouthful, and then another. The flask hadn't been full and was more than half empty by now. The New Englander kept the rest for himself, putting his horse out in front once more and slugging from the flask. It was mighty peculiar-tasting brandy, but a man in the redwoods can't afford to be too fussy about what chance sends his way in the line of beverages.

The horses began giving Silas trouble, and he couldn't seem to sort them out anymore. Finally, all progress stopped when the last horse caught the lariat in a young fir and twisted it around the trunk and branches in trying to get free. In his efforts to untangle the animal, Silas only made things worse. He threw the empty silver flask aside and dismounted. As he swung down out of the saddle, he lost his balance and sat on the ground bewildered. His eyes had a glazed, faraway look, and he mumbled incoherently to Draper.

"Be glad to help you, friend," One-Ear said, swinging his leg over the saddle and stepping down from the stirrup, his hands still bound behind him. He stepped through his bound wrists and now had his hands in front of his body.

Silas tried weakly to stop him from pulling the bowie from his belt. Draper cut the rawhide thong Raider had used to bind his wrists but didn't bother to take the gun from Silas's holster. His own gunbelt and weapon were on Silas's saddle, and these he fetched, along with the silver flask, which he held tauntingly in front of the helpless New Englander.

Draper freed his horse from the lariat. "Know what was in that brandy, friend? Opium. Mixed in a tincture like this, they call it laudanum. Be careful of it, friend," Draper said, jumping into his saddle. "It's been the ruin of many a good man."

CHAPTER FOUR

When Silas Hanks came out of his stupor and realized he had let One-Ear Draper escape, he thought about heading back to Maine in a hurry in order not to have to face Raider. Silas was a tough son of a gun, but he saw himself as a milksop compared to the Pinkerton. He fully expected that Raider would maim him in some way, as an example to others not to foul up. But he decided not to run, only because that would make things worse by making it look like he had been in cahoots with One-Ear. A mistake was one thing—treachery was another. He had made a mistake, he had been a fool—but that was all. Silas Hanks was no back-stabber. He would stand his ground and defend his name....

The big Maine woodsman was more than surprised by Raider's reaction to his story when the Pinkerton returned to the sawmill after safely delivering the payroll to the logging camp. Raider was intensely interested in

One-Ear's flask of laudanum and how One-Ear had re-
trieved the empty flask before he left.

"Where can you buy laudanum in these parts?"
Raider wanted to know.

"There's a drugstore in Mendocino City, the one at
the south end of Main Street, which will sell you all you
want," Cal Blair said. "I guess most any drugstore in
any town can supply you. And some of the Chinamen
hereabouts smoke opium. Crewmen bring it up from
San Francisco on the schooners and sell it to them."

Silas was still waiting for Raider to explode, at the
very least to cuss him out and knock him down. Instead,
Raider seemed strangely subdued, as if it was he who
was in the wrong, not Silas.

Finally Raider said to him, "I ain't gonna criticize a
man for drinking a little brandy out in the woods, especially not after he took the precaution of having his prisoner drink from it first. A man couldn't reasonably
expect someone to be hardened to that laudanum stuff
and function good with it in his system, while another
man would sit on his ass with drool running down his
chin."

"You hear about that in the cities," Cal Blair put in,
"but not up here in the redwoods."

"If he's taking that stuff, he's gonna have to stay
close to some supply," Raider said. "It won't be that
easy to catch him again, though, not now that he knows
I'm here. He don't seem too smart when you're talking
with him, but he's sharp as a whip when it comes to
sliding away from trouble."

"Yeah, I reckon," Silas opined, amazed how calmly
Raider was taking things.

"Him and me go way back," the Pinkerton went on.

"About six or seven years ago, I hunted him down for train robbing down in Kansas. I chased him across Pottawatomie County before I gunned down a pard of his and took him prisoner with flesh wounds in his arm and leg. The nearest town was Emmett, and I left him with the marshal there while I went to Topeka to arrange his transport. Draper had a fight with the town drunk in jail and killed him. A crowd of locals arrived at the jail to string him up while the marshal was away. Draper tricked them into taking a drunk cowboy in his stead and slipped out while they were lynching him. It was nearly two years before the Pinkertons heard about him again."

"Where was that?"

"Grand Junction, Colorado," Raider answered. "I went there and found no trace of him. I guessed he had moved on. Then about a year after that, the agency located him in Billings, Montana. An informer telegraphed where we could find him. I got the drop on him in a saloon and walked him to the railroad station without letting him even pick up his things at the hotel. We had to travel overnight to Cheyenne and change trains there for Kansas. We had a carriage to ourselves, so I cuffed him to the iron armrest of a single seat and stretched out on a bench myself to catch some shut-eye. When I woke up, him and the seat was gone. The bastard had unscrewed it from the floor and jumped off the moving train, holding it in his hands. I often thought about what he must have looked like—this dude carrying a heavy wood-and-iron train seat across the empty prairies."

They all laughed at that.

"So how come you trusted me to take him in?" Silas asked.

"That was my mistake," Raider conceded with a grin. "He was so easy to catch, I forgot how hard he is to hold."

"So what happens now?" Cal wanted to know.

"I'm going after him."

Cal frowned. "With all due respect, Raider, I brought you out here to look out for the Eagle Timber Company, not hunt down your old enemies. Sure, One-Ear Draper is part of my problem, but he's only part. What happens to us after you take off?"

"I'm not going anyplace until my backup man arrives. He'll be here in a day or two. That'll free me to take care of One-Ear. This fella killed your brother, Cal. I'd say he was a great part of your problem."

"Yeah, I'd like to stake the bastard to the ground and slowly peel off his skin with a bowie knife," Cal said venomously. "That'd be sweet vengeance. But I'd be kidding myself if I thought that was taking care of the big problem. One-Ear Draper ain't the one trying to put us out of business. He wasn't the one who ordered Abe's death. That's the man I want you to get."

Stanton skimmed over the calm water in his small sailboat. He was more than twenty miles down the coast when he spotted Point Arena to the south. His destination was just north of the point to a doghole called Manchester. He sailed in close to the long sandy beach, dropped the mainsail, lowered an anchor fore and aft, then went ashore by dinghy. Having followed a wagon train inland a few hundred yards, he came to a two-story log house with a large porch along two sides of it. A man sat in a wicker chair on the porch, reading a newspaper. Stanton hailed him.

The man looked up, and an expression of annoyance crossed his face. He called, "What is it now, Stanton?"

"I don't think it's something you'd want me to shout across to you," Stanton called back.

The man beckoned to him, picked up a small brass hand bell on a table, and rang it. The maid appeared as Stanton sat himself in a chair.

"Coffee," the man ordered, "and any cold meat and bread you can find in the kitchen."

"Yes, sir." She left them.

Stanton began, "Mr. Dench—"

Jeff Dench held up a wide hand with thick fingers, perfectly manicured, for silence. He was dressed city-style, and he was shaved and barbered. But tailoring and grooming did not hide the power of his body and his overbearing personality.

"I'm not in the mood for a collection of excuses or a long list of complaints, Stanton. Make it short. Tell me what went wrong and how you intend to fix it."

"One-Ear Draper let us down again, sir. But that's not why I came. One-Ear is hiding out. He's running scared of a Pinkerton named Raider, who was hired on by Cal Blair. You ain't never met One-Ear. If you had, you'd be plumb surprised at the notion of him being scared by anyone. Since it seems like we might have some real opposition with Raider, I thought I'd check him out with you before going any further."

Dench nodded. "A wise move, Stanton. I agree. I'll send word by boat tonight to have someone at my San Francisco office see what they can find on him. But I think maybe your friend One-Ear has gone soft. That's a thing can happen to any man. This is the second payroll he's missed out on. This fella Raider wasn't around for the first, was he?"

"No."

"So let's see just how mean and smart this Pinkerton is," Dench said. "Hire some guns and throw them at him. See what happens."

"You don't think we should ease up for a spell?" Stanton asked in a tone that made it plain that he did.

"Naw. Let's see what this Pinkerton is made of."

The maid arrived with the food and coffee.

Abe Blair had left a childless widow. She lived close by Cal Blair's house. Cal had a wife and three small kids. The two women never did get along. Although Cal's wife tried to comfort Brenda, Abe's widow, it didn't work well, and soon the two were politely avoiding one another as usual. Brenda was friends with the Little River schoolmarm and the postmistress and one or two merchants' wives in Mendocino City. She visited them or was called on by one of them nearly every day, but her nights were long and lonely in that silent house.

Being an attractive woman, with green eyes, long black hair, and a full body, she caught Raider's eye. Seeing her wearing black for mourning and knowing of course who she was, he held back from approaching her, other than raising his hat to her and smiling at her whenever they chanced to pass. It wasn't that Raider had any great respect for a widow's privacy or any belief in mourning the dead. He just didn't know how to go about letting her know what he wanted without causing insult or offense.

Now if Doc Weatherbee were around, he would have

kidded her into believing he was interested in her soul, even while he had a hand on her knee. Raider knew he didn't have that easy way about him. Women just looked him in the eye and they knew right away what he had in mind! He never could fool them with sweet talk.

Yet she looked at him in a flirtatious way—and once he thought he saw a blush creep into her cheeks when she saw him coming. He couldn't be sure. One night he went around to her house. It was pitch dark, except for the lamp glow behind a blind in her window. He imagined her sitting there alone. Worried about frightening her, he walked silently up to the front door, intending to knock quietly and go away if she didn't respond immediately. He was fairly sober and guessed he was about to make a fool of himself somehow. First sign of things going wrong, he would run. She would never know who had been there.

He was near the door, not making a sound, when he caught his boot in one of those dangfool little iron hoops women stick in the ground around flowers. Falling full length on some thorny rosebushes, he forgot about being quiet and decent. After shouting obscenities in a recent widow's garden and trampling the flowers she was no doubt growing to put on her husband's grave, Raider decided it might be better to delay this visit. He went off into the dark, pulling thorns from his skin.

Brenda was afraid he might have heard her laughing from inside the house. She was an independent woman, yet terrified to be alone. Imaginary footsteps on floorboards, closet doors squeaking open by themselves, scratching on windowpanes, her cat staring as if alarmed at a dark doorway—these things made her heart skip a beat, and she would put her hand out for the Winchester rifle she kept within reach.

Her hearing having been made acute by her lonely nervousness, she went to an unlit window with her rifle when she thought she recognized the sound of boot leather on a stone somewhere in front of the house. She almost screamed when she noticed a dark form moving out there. Then, for an instant, Raider's face was caught in the subdued lamp glow from the window. Brenda felt herself change. Her heart was still racing, but it was not from fear now but from a much more pleasurable feeling.

Then he fell and cursed and walked off into the night. She had laughed. Up until now, she had been a bit afraid of him—she saw how Cal and the sawmill workers treated him with wary respect. Now she saw a vulnerable side of him. She wanted him to come in, and was disappointed after he left.

In a little while, she became annoyed with herself for thinking about a stranger like this. She was ashamed of her desires. Grass hadn't grown yet on her husband's grave and she was already flirting with a new man.

Raider had a job to do, and he meant to get it done. He was not going to get it done by chasing the wife of one of the men who had hired him and who was now dead. So Raider kept away from where the widow lived and didn't go to places where he was likely to run into her during the day, such as the stores in Little River. He really had two jobs to do: one, take care of things at the timber company; two, nail Draper. He would have to put Draper out of his mind until his Pinkerton colleague arrived. In the meantime, he intended to run things so that peace and quiet prevailed.

No matter how good Raider's intentions were, he never did have much of a talent for peace and quiet. Of course, that wasn't the way *he* saw it. He saw himself besieged with desk-bound know-nothings who took pleasure in unloading their paperwork on him. It was only natural that he would blow up now and again, and settle things with the gun rather than the pen. If men could be governed by paperwork alone, there would be no need for Pinkertons in the first place!

For a man like Raider, law and order was a personal thing. He wasn't part of any system. He couldn't be — even if he tried. It was a one-on-one thing for him, person against person. Draper might as well have spat in lf002his face as escape from his custody. All these years it had been rankling Raider that One-Ear had gone free. Had the Pinkertons not been willing to send him after Draper — as they had — he would have gone on his own time and spent his own money, not from wanting so much to see the law prevail as to settle a private score.

A Pinkerton's role was an ambiguous one. He belonged not to a nationwide law enforcement agency, although this was as often as not their unofficial duty west of the Mississippi, but to a private detective agency. The Pinkerton operative had the right to take in the perpetrators of a certain crime, or specific wanted individuals. In theory, he had no cause to interfere in a train robbery if he was assigned to hunt cattle rustlers. Out west, things didn't work like that, and an operative had to use his own discretion. In this matter of personal judgment, Raider very rarely took the same view as his agency superiors in Chicago. Of course, they didn't know this most of the time, since he sent in so few written reports.

Allan Pinkerton controlled his operatives nationwide through his inflexible rules and regulations. Every man had to keep Chicago headquarters informed in writing on the latest developments of a case and justify in detail every penny spent on expenses. This system worked well for the agency's founder—at any given time he could tell almost exactly what was happening wherever he had operatives.

The only drawback to this system became evident when well-drilled, obedient operatives were just not mean enough and sharp-witted enough to handle some extra-raw badmen. Allan Pinkerton had to quietly allow some hell-raising rule-breakers into his agency as operatives to handle the rough cases, although he never admitted this openly and never eased up in his efforts to discipline these men. Raider was the legendary member of this small group.

The town of Little River was much smaller than Mendocino City, which in turn was a fairly small town itself. But if Mendocino City was not a city by eastern standards, it sure packed in more action and entertainment than most dull metropolises twenty times its size. When the residents of Little River felt like raising more hell than usual or wanted to find a real party gal, they took themselves a few miles north to their bigger neighbor.

Raider was making this journey on a borrowed horse, along with Silas Hanks and some other loggers, and was skirting the base of a pine-covered hill when a rifle shot rang out. The bullet missed. The men lost no time in jumping from their saddles and taking cover behind their horses as they pulled them into the trees for cover. The shot had been fired from among the pines, partway up the hill. A telltale small cloud of blue smoke hung in the air. By now the gunman was probably making good his escape—or looking for another vantage point.

"That was meant for me," Raider said. "I reckon I'm dangerous company to be around. You men go on while I go up the hillside and see if I can find that dry-gulcher."

"No way," Silas told him. "You stay here and watch the trail, Raider, while we go up. We cut these paths through this timber. We know them better than some out-of-town back-shooter. We'll flush him out of these trees down to you in no time. Come on, boys."

The loggers mounted, drew their guns, and spurred their horses uphill on a narrow trail into the timber. They split up along various branches and shouted to one another to reveal their locations in the dense trees. Raider listened to them from the main trail at the base of the hill and watched for the sudden emergence of his assailant. He held his .30–30 Winchester carbine at the ready and walked up and down, never straying too far from where his horse was tied in case he had to give chase. He heard a shot partway up the hill and more shouts, coming closer all the time. A horse and rider came through the undergrowth in a hurry—Raider heard them before he saw them. He raised the carbine to his shoulder.

When the man rode out onto the trail, the first thing he looked into was the carbine's muzzle. His eyes darted wildly from side to side, as if he was thinking about making a break for it. The carbine barrel re-

mained leveled unwaveringly at his head. The man
scowled and pulled on the reins to stop his horse. The
Winchester barrel dipped a couple of times, indicating
that he was to get down off his horse. Once he was off,
Raider lowered the carbine to his hip and, keeping him
covered, approached the horse. With his left hand, he
felt the man's rifle barrel in its saddle scabbard. It was
still warm from the ambush shot the man had fired.

Raider took his time about bringing back his left
hand to support his carbine, giving the man a chance to
draw his revolver if he had a mind to. But the man was
likely too scared or else saw through Raider's maneuver,
guessing that he could manage a carbine one-handed
well enough to count at this distance.

"Ain't I seen you somewhere before?" Raider asked
him.

The other loggers arrived before the man could reply.
One deliberately jostled him with his horse and nearly
knocked him to the ground. They were all aware that
the man still carried his six-gun and had not been disarmed by Raider. They hoped to see some fun yet. Silas
Hanks began tying a noose in a length of rope.

"You seen me last night in Little River," the man
shouted over to Raider. He moved closer to the Pinkerton who showed more inclination to talk and maybe rep-
resented a better hope for his future than these mounted
woodsmen.

Raider looked at the beads of sweat rolling down the
man's narrow forehead. He had lost his hat, which revealed that he had lost much of his hair. Raider asked
him, "Who sent you looking for me?"

"Who said I was looking for you?"

"Because you shot at me," Raider answered. "And if

you say you didn't shoot at me, you better explain who it was you were trying to hit."

"A fella paid me to blast you. Gave me fifty dollars in gold, said I'd collect another fifty after the job. I don't know his name. I came into Little River last night so I could get a look at you."

"You're full of shit," Raider growled. "First of all, if some fool paid you fifty in advance to do something, he'd never lay eyes on you again. But supposing you did take fifty in advance to do the killing, how could you pick up the other fifty after the job if you didn't know who had hired you?"

"I never thought of that," the man said lamely.

"And how did you know I was going to be coming this way?" Raider asked. "I didn't know myself until a few hours ago. No, you was waiting here for some other reason and I just chanced along. Why were you here?"

"I figured you'd be going to Mendocino City pretty soon."

"So you were willing to sit up here in the trees for maybe a few days so you could take a shot at me? You ain't no marksman. You ain't even a good liar."

"I got the rope ready," Silas announced.

"I wanna see him swing," another logger shouted.

"Put him on his horse," a third lumberjack suggested.

The man turned to Raider in a panic. "A Pinkerton don't allow that to happen to people!"

"So you know I'm a Pinkerton," Raider murmured. He let the loggers put a bit of feeling in their lynching party before he finally said, "Hold it, boys. I think this here fella has a right to die like a man."

They all looked at the six-gun on the man's hip and

urged their horses out of the line of fire, leaving only him and Raider facing each other on the trail, maybe six paces apart.

"I don't want this," the man said, his voice kind of croaky.

"You can either talk or fight," Raider said in a voice so calm and slow its eerie sound made the hackles stand up on the back of the man's neck.

"I don't wanna die," he whined.

"Then you better be faster than me," Raider said by way of kindly advice.

"Fella who hired me is named Stanton," the frightened man blurted out.

"I know him," Silas called from the side. "I could believe it."

"You let me go now? I swear not to come back."

"You don't have to promise me anything," Raider told him with a smile. "If I was to let you go, I'd be doing the promising to you—like putting a piece of lead between your eyes if I saw you north of San Francisco again. Believe me, you don't have to promise me a thing. But I ain't letting you go as easy as that, not after you tried to kill me."

"I'll tell you something else. Something important. Will you let me go then?"

Raider thought about that for a moment. "I'd like to keep you chained to a log at the sawmill until I was ready to go back down the coast again. It wouldn't be more than a month or two. Then I'd find you a proper jail where you'd be in out of the weather and these loggers couldn't kick you all the time as they passed by. But it would have to be something real important for me to let you ride free."

"It is." The man was shivering now as well as sweating. "You notice those two dudes who was in the Skid Row last night? One had a ginger beard and a broken nose—that's Red Danny. The other one had gray hair, though he's young, and black eyebrows that kind of look odd. That's the Kid, that's what he calls hisself. They're with me, hired by Stanton to kill you. They was to get you when you walked in the door of the Skid Row today. Give you no warning, just gun you down and run out the door. They was to ride north to Mendocino City and get on a boat that's leaving tonight for San Francisco. My job was to cover their retreat in case anyone chased after them from Little River. Then I could join them later at the wharf. The boat captain has our money. He don't know what it's for—only not to give it to us until he gets a message. I reckon Stanton would've sent someone after he heard the news about your, eh—"

"Who are you?" Raider asked.

"They know me as Richmond."

"Okay, Richmond, I'm a man who keeps my promises. I'll let you go. You're free to do as you like, but if I was you, I'd ride hell for leather to Mendocino City, get rid of that horse and saddle, then get on that boat. Me and these boys are headed that way. I won't kill you if I find you on that boat. I will if you're on dry land. That's a promise."

The loggers looked after him in a disappointed way as he galloped north.

Silas asked, "You really going to let him go?"

Raider nodded. "If you boys would be kind enough to ride back with me to a certain saloon in Little River, I'll buy each man jack of you a bottle of whiskey for himself when we get to Mendocino City later on."

* * *

Raider saw the window of the storeroom in back of the Skid Row saloon open. Silas stuck his head out and beckoned him.

"They're both here, " Silas said. "They're not together, nicely spread out, just watching the door. Their horses are tied to the hitching rail outside. Maybe that little rat was telling the truth."

"He was frightened enough to," Raider said as he squeezed his large frame in the open window. He stood with Silas among the stacked crates and barrels, loosened his Remington in its holster, then opened the storeroom door a crack. Red Danny was standing with his back to the bar, an untouched whiskey bottle at his elbow. His eyes never left the street door. The Kid had his back to a wall, a drink in his left hand, pretending to be watching a card game but facing the street door.

"You sure you don't—" Silas began.

"Thanks, Silas, but this is my show." Raider eased the door open and stepped out into the saloon. He had already made a decision on one thing—the Kid looked like he would be the faster of the two. Raider moved unseen by them to a more favorable position. He stood for a few moments, feet apart, hands by his sides, balancing on the balls of his feet. He waited for a lull in the bar talk, then said in a loud clear voice, "Kid, Danny, Richmond sent me."

He saw their bodies stiffen as they realized they had been betrayed—that their victim was not going to walk in from the street unawares, that instead he was already behind them and calling them by name. They whirled about simultaneously, each bringing his revolver out of its holster and thumbing the hammer back.

Raider's right hand dropped and lifted up his long-barreled Remington .44 with his finger tightly pressed down on the trigger. The heel of his left hand fanned back the hammer, which snapped back on the firing pin while Raider aimed the barrel at the Kid. Each of the Pinkerton's shots had to hit home—there would be no time for second tries. Through the flame and smoke, Raider saw the left side of the Kid's shirt crumble. He had no time to see anything else, because he was already putting the barrel on the big ginger-bearded man with the broken nose, who stood back to the bar about to blast a shot at him.

The heel of Raider's left hand brushed back the hammer once more, just enough for the chambers to revolve and a fresh cartridge to come under the firing pin. The hammer crashed down and the barrel spat out its hot lump of flying death.

The bullet hit Red Danny on the left cheekbone, just above where his beard started. His finger was pressing the trigger as the lead projectile impacted on his face bone. The shock of the bullet's impact caused his gun hand to jerk, although it didn't come in time to prevent his finger from pressing home.

As Raider's .44-caliber slug crushed his cheekbone and flattened against his skull before shattering it, his gun discharged. The bullet sailed over Raider's left shoulder and buried itself in the wall.

The light died in Red Danny's eyes as his bullet went astray. No one would ever know whether he had seen his bullet miss the Pinkerton. If he hadn't, it would have saved him from dying a disappointed man.

The Kid lay on his side in the sawdust on the saloon

floor. The only thing moving about him was the steady flow of blood on his shirtfront.

The shootings in Little River delayed Raider and the loggers for little more than an hour on their trip to Mendocino City. The Little River marshal could see no cause to hold any man for questioning who handled two adversaries at the same time after giving them a warning. That kind of courtesy was not common in the redwoods country.

When they reached Mendocino City, Silas Hanks asked Raider, "You going down to see if Richmond is on that ship?"

"Hell, no," Raider responded. "I might end up shooting the rat if I did. I've had enough for one day. Come on in this place and I'll buy each of you that bottle. Allan Pinkerton is going to choke when I charge it to expenses, which should make that whiskey taste all the better. I been meaning to ask you, Silas, about this Stanton who you said you knew."

They went into a huge, brightly lit saloon. A fiddler and an accordion player were sawing out some waltzes and polkas on a stand in one corner. A few couples staggered around together between the tables, like they might be dancing. There was a fistfight when one man bumped against a gaming table and knocked some playing cards on the floor.

"Stanton worked as a clerk for some of the timber companies," Silas said. "One place missed some petty cash, another was charged for supplies never delivered, something else was missing someplace else—it was the same story wherever he worked. Word got around, and in the end no one would hire him. Since that time, he's been shipping in supplies from San Francisco, paying for them on the barrel head and reselling them hereabouts to loggers. When we have a spell of rough weather and the schooners can't bring in fresh supplies, he can raise his prices on what he's got and make big money. Otherwise, I think he makes a modest living but an honest one. His trouble is he likes to gamble, so no matter how good his business is, he's always short of cash and willing to do nearly anything for easy money."

"Like what?" Raider wanted to know.

"They say Stanton was involved in a timber rights swindle a few years ago. A fella from San Francisco ended up with all the rights on a large tract for very little money. Stanton was flush for a while after that. Then there was trouble over some sawmill down in Manchester, and Stanton pulled a fast one there, too. Fella up by Fort Bragg beat him so bad a few years ago he left him for dead. But Stanton came round. All the same, he didn't bother that fella none after that. My guess is that he'd d've been afraid of Abe and Cal Blair. Them two could look after theirselves. Leastways I never seen Stanton skulking around here."

"What does he own around here?"

"Not a thing," Silas said. "He rents a shed to store the goods that come up by schooner from the city. I think he lives mostly in hotels. And he blows everything at the gaming tables. He plays everything—roulette, faro, poker, dice, you name it."

"He doesn't sound to me like he's the one trying to take over the Eagle Timber Company for himself," Raider said.

"No," Silas agreed, "but he might be working for the man who is."

They left off talking about serious things then and paid some closer attention to what was around them. Raider still had Abe's widow, Brenda, on his mind. Yet it wasn't until after Silas jokingly remarked about it that Raider realized the woman he had picked for himself bore a remarkable resemblance to the widow.

"What's it to me who she looks like?" Raider snapped, annoyed at Silas for what he had guessed at and at himself for being so unaware of what he was doing.

Silas smirked knowingly, then turned his attentions to a little Mexican firecracker about half his height but who could match him drink for drink and cuss for cuss.

Brenda's look-alike was called Iris. She had managed to overhear Silas's remarks in the noisy saloon, and now she wanted to know about the woman she looked like and asked Raider if he was in love with this woman. Raider blushed. Damn it, he had come here to have a good time—not to be harassed and asked dumb questions. Seeing him flustered, Iris persisted. She only eased up when it looked like Raider might walk out the door and go down the street to another place.

They did some dancing and had some fun. Then they left the saloon and climbed up a muddy, rutted street to where she lived, in a small cabin constructed partly from logs and partly from driftwood. The cabin was on the edge of town, almost in the forest.

"I like it this way," Iris said. "Nobody comes out this far to bother me when I don't want to be bothered—they can always find someone closer in town. Anyway I came up here to get away from crowds and streets, but a woman can't live alone in the woods like a man can.

Else I might have been a trapper—no, I'd feel sorry for those poor animals in the traps—maybe a prospector. Yeah, I'd like that. You a gunman?"

"Sort of."

"I knew. You have that look about you. Killed anyone lately?"

"Sure. Two already today. Down in Little River."

She laughed, clearly not believing him. She would be surprised, when she heard tomorrow. As well as about the sort of gunman he was.

Iris undressed in front of him, looking at the bulge in front of his pants to make sure she was exciting him. Raider watched her slowly part her long legs as she reclined naked on the bed, watching him watch her. His eyes greedily roved over the soft skin of her smooth thighs, traced the sensuous lines of her hips and ass, gazed at the tangle of dark hair over her sex.

He unbuckled his gunbelt and let it drop to the board floor. He kicked off one boot, then the other, not taking his eyes away from her voluptuous body. The rest of his clothes came off like maple leaves in a big wind. His big cock stuck out in front of him. She smiled at the sight of it and licked her lips.

Raider got down between her legs and ran his tongue along the smooth insides of her thighs, all the way up to her pussy. He tongued her lips, excited her clit with the tip of his tongue, tantalizing her and rousing her to higher levels of excitement. Then he pushed the full length of his muscular tongue into her writhing, trembling interior.

With long, lingering strokes, his tongue poked deep

into her most sensitive tissues, sending white-hot flames of pleasure flickering through her body.

She grabbed his head with both hands and pulled his face hard into her, screaming as she came, convulsed in ecstasy by his master touch.

CHAPTER FIVE

"Your new partner arrived last night," Cal Blair informed Raider next morning at the Little River sawmill. "Ted Malloy happened to be with me here, going over some accounts, when he walked in. Malloy found him a place to stay, and last I saw of them they were in the church social hall playing chess."

Raider's mouth dropped open. All he could say was, "What have they sent me this time?"

"A real promising young man." Cal grinned sardonically. "I'd have given him a job myself in the accounts department."

"A fucking bookkeeper," Raider grated. "You know why they sent him? To run a check on my expenses. I put my life on the line, and all they worry about is a few stray dollars spent on whiskey and women. I can't even afford to gamble very often."

Cal smiled. "I wouldn't say this young man is much of a gambler, womanizer, or drinker."

"Fucking chess. I don't believe it."

"You have no control over who they send out as your partner?"

Raider shook his head. "Chicago has dumped some real blanks on me before. I've even lost a few—they thought they were out for a stroll in the park and walked into some bullets."

"It sounds cruel to send inexperienced young men into dangerous situations."

"It's even crueler on me," Raider muttered. He suddenly brightened. "If a customer strongly objects to a particular operative and has reasonable grounds for doing so, Chicago will be willing to withdraw him at no cost to the customer. I say we have Malloy put his pal on a boat back to San Francisco today, with a telegram for Mr. Pinkerton."

"Not so fast, Raider," Cal objected. "Over the years a lot of men have worked for me and my brother. I've learned that some of the most unlikely ones turn out the best. It ain't fair to turn a man away without giving him a chance. Besides, I'm a chess player myself. I don't hold that against any man."

"Being a Pinkerton ain't a job for dreamy intellectuals," Raider told him. "If a man don't work out as a logger, you can let him go and no harm done. If he don't work out as a Pinkerton, some innocent folk are liable to be killed before he's retired from the scene. I hope you don't have to learn that the hard way. Enough bad things have happened here. We don't need no—"

"Give him a chance, Raider."

"I ain't even seen the little bastard. I may kick his butt and send him home to his mother."

Samuel Trotter was reading aloud from an opera review in a San Francisco newspaper when Raider came into Ted Malloy's office. Raider looked over the small-framed young man, who was wearing thick spectacles and city clothes. Malloy tried to introduce them.

"Trotter? That's your name?" Raider said, cutting Malloy's preamble short. "All right, Trotter. Come with me. I want you to meet some of the men and see the machines you're here to protect."

The men poling the logs in the storage pond either guffawed or looked amazed when Raider informed them that Trotter was here to see they came to no harm. It was the same at the sawmill. Trotter saw no humor in the situation. He just gazed around him absentmindedly. The men were too afraid of Raider to give Trotter a hard time while he was looking on. But Raider fixed it nicely so that as soon as he turned his back, Trotter was bound to hit some heavy going.

Whenever Samuel Trotter was seen around the compound for the rest of that day, the timber workers went out of their way to kid him. At first the ribbing was good-natured, but when Trotter took everything they threw at him in a vague professional way, the workers' efforts grew more challenging and ham-fisted. The men riding the massive redwood logs in the storage pond saw that he got wet from head to toe. Those making shingles from the bark sent wood chips flying his way with the speed of bullets—and grew impatient when the young Pinkerton seemed to fail to notice them through his thick lenses. The men cutting posts and planks with big table saws walked him within inches of whirring blades —nothing seemed to faze him. Workers handing planks near the chute reswung them close to his head. Through it all, Samuel Trotter wandered in a mild daze, as if he were looking for something but could not quite remember what.

Emboldened by the fact that Raider was leaving the new man to his own devices, letting him fend for himself, some of the saw operators staged a spectacle for Trotter's benefit. Having first made sure that Raider and Cal Blair had left the compound to go into Little River for a spell, two of them tied bandannas over their faces and chased a third with axes, taking wild swings at him as he shouted for help in mock terror. The other workers did nothing to interfere, trying to keep their faces straight while they yelled, "Intruders!"

When Trotter rushed to the scene to investigate, the man being chased headed for him and tried to hide behind him, although he was almost twice Trotter's size, pleading, "Protect me! Save me!"

The two men with the axes swung the steel blades menacingly and whooped as they approached. It was a fairly realistic performance, considering none of the three men had any experience in the theater, although they had all seen bloodthirsty melodramas put on by touring companies.

No one ever noticed Trotter pick up the seven-foot length of two-inch-by-two timber. He jabbed one end of it in the nearest axman's gut, which brought the fellow to his knees. Next he stepped to the side while he swung the other end of the timber around, neatly catching the second axman across the nose. A sharp rap on the back of his skull caused him to drop his ax.

Meanwhile the first axman was getting to his feet, trying to explain to Trotter this was all a joke. Trotter poleaxed him with the length of timber, and gave him another full swing while he was down in order to keep him there.

When the man they had been chasing tried to intervene on their behalf, Trotter downed him, too. Then he walloped the second axman a couple of times across the back because he moved without permission.

When Raider and Cal returned, they found the workers in a group trying to calm Trotter down. The little Pinkerton had got himself all riled up and was proving difficult to soothe.

Trotter said to Raider, "These clowns are lucky I decided I had no need to use my gun on them." He lifted his vest to reveal a nickel-plated Colt Third Model .41 derringer. For some reason, everyone had assumed that Samuel Trotter was unarmed—as well as unable to take care of himself.

Raider shook his head at the workers gathered about. "I don't know what you boys think you're up to. You know you don't go messing with a Pinkerton."

He walked away with Cal, who said to him, "Looks like I was right, Raider, in wanting to keep him on the job."

Raider wasn't going to admit that easily that he might have been wrong. "Like you say, we'll keep him for a tryout."

"I been checking into Stanton," Cal Blair told Raider and Samuel Trotter as they put away a meal of grilled salmon and spinach at an eating house in Little River. "I've already told you I do business with him whenever there's a shortage of something he has in stock. His prices are high, but when you need something you have to have it, regardless of cost. I've no complaints about my dealings with him, and I ain't heard of none from others, either. The only bad talk I hear about him concerns him setting himself up as a middleman for outsiders."

"You find out for who?" Raider asked.

"Yes, I did, and that's what's interesting," Cal went on. "I think you might have put me onto who's after the Eagle Timber Company. Stanton's done bits and pieces for just about anyone who would front him some money. But that's all these deals have amounted to—bits and pieces. About four years ago, however, he became involved in that big timber rights swindle that Silas Hanks told you about. Maybe a year after that, he was in on the Manchester sawmill deal, where the owner was practically run off his own property because he owed some loans. The fella Stanton was fronting for in both deals is Jeff Dench. He made a fortune when the City of San Francisco built over some no-good marshland he owned on the bay."

"Is he the one who owns the Dench Construction Company?" Raider asked.

"That's him. You know him?"

"No, I only seen his men working in San Francisco —pounding nails and sawing wood like they was building the ark with storm clouds gathering."

"It's only natural a man in the construction business would know the value of lumber and want to get his hands on his own private supply," Cal said. "But us lumbermen don't want no builders in our business. We want to sell wood to them, not have them cut their own.

So he used Stanton so we wouldn't know he was buying the timber rights near here. There wasn't nothing illegal about that. It made us plenty mad at Stanton, but we got over it. That wasn't all Stanton done. He hired some drifters to set a fire on the land. Then he bribed a lawyer for the owners to write to them back east, enclosing a newspaper clipping about the fire, as if their timberland was a total loss, advising them to sell it for anything they could get. They sold it to Stanton for next to nothing."

"But there really was a fire," Trotter put in.

"Sure. A full-scale forest fire. But there ain't a big redwood standing that hasn't survived several forest fires. The flames burn up the small and the average-size trees and they scar the outsides of the big redwoods, but that's all. The fires help the redwoods by adding charcoal to the soil. Some tanbark, fir, and pines were lost, that was all. Anyway, Stanton transferred the ownership to Dench a couple of days later, and everything was all sewed up before any of us sawmill owners heard a word about what was going on. The lawyer got run out of town. Stanton stayed. After a while, when we ran short on something that we knew he had, we forgot we had sworn not to give him our business anymore."

"Then he fronted for Dench at the Manchester sawmill," Raider prompted.

"Right. We had been expecting him to build his own mill here at Little River, so my brother and me were kind of surprised when he bought in down there. He can't use any of the trees up here that far down the coast—it wouldn't pay to run the trees there when they could be milled here. But I see now that he was taking the long view. I been told he's been clear-cutting at such a rate down there his concession will be bare of trees in a few years' time. Now I'm thinking maybe he's picked out his next sawmill, nice and close to the timberland he controls up here. So happens that mill is mine."

"You could be right," Raider agreed. "Have you ever met Dench?"

"He comes up this way once or twice a year," Cal said, "buying timber. He's been doing that for years. He always stopped by my brother and me, and most times he bought from us. He knew we were dependable and that we'd deliver him quality. That's more than you can say for a lot of people on this coast."

"So he knows you and this place fairly well," Raider murmured as if to himself.

"Jeff Dench? Sure he does. He'd stay over in Abe's house for the night when he came, on account of Abe not having kids and so having more room in the house and all."

Raider mumbled, "I'm gonna nail the son of a bitch."

Seven span of oxen pulled twelve logs, chained end to end to each other like railroad cars, down a steep skid road through forest some miles inland from the coast. A sugler ran alongside the logs, pouring brook water from a bucket on their path to make them slide more easily. The bull team strained and jostled in wood yokes and chains, driven onward by the curses and blows of the bullpuncher. In the forest, he had no room to use a bull-whip and instead used a sharply pointed stick as a goad. At a hundred dollars a month, bullpunchers earned more than any other worker in the redwoods.

As the bull team and their burden came downhill, the

logs began to slide more quickly. The bullpuncher yelled back at the dogger to put on the brakes—made from chains—on the logs to slow them down. The rear span of oxen was often crushed when overrun by logs. The dogger slowed the logs' downward slide, while the bullpuncher cussed and goaded the fourteen animals to a faster pace. At the end of the incline the team came to a long level stretch, and as the logs came off the slope, the oxen felt the pull of their load and strained forward in their harness.

Here the skid road was built over marshy ground and was raised several feet above the mud. Round about, the stumps of giant trees showed where loggers had worked ten or fifteen years before. These days, most of the big redwoods close to the coast had been felled, and the skid roads grew longer every year as the logging camps moved farther inland.

The lead oxen began to balk at one point along the level stretch, not far before a bend. Only the savage goading and kicks of the bullpuncher kept them moving ahead as they twisted their yoked heads from side to side, looking to escape since they were not allowed to stop. The bullpuncher's shouts brought Raider and Silas Hanks from around the bend.

"They smell the dead flesh," Raider called to the bullpuncher. "You might as well ease up on them. They ain't going anywheres for a few hours yet."

The team was allowed to come to a halt, and the bullpuncher shouted back to Raider, "Another blow-out?"

"Right. Lost one man and half a team. I wasn't expecting you or I'd have come to escort you. Didn't you meet the rider?"

"Sure I met him. I told him what I'm gonna tell you—I don't need no escort. I can take care of myself. Who was killed?"

Raider answered, "Jerry Carpenter."

"He warn't no good anyhow. He won't be missed."

Silas put in angrily, "He was a better man than you."

"That may be, but he warn't a better bullpuncher, and that's what counts in these here redwoods."

Silas laughed. "I always said you was part grizzly bear."

Indeed the bullpuncher had a lumbering bearlike walk. The bulky man looked capable of stoving in a cabin door with a swing of a mighty paw. The look on his face was as mean and savage as any grizzly's, and he was just about as ugly. Leaving the sugler and dogger to care for the team, he followed Raider and Silas around the bend, from where the sounds of men working could be heard.

A dozen or so workers were filling in a crater in the skid road, laying a pair of long narrow pine trunks across it lengthwise with the direction of the road and placing shorter crosspieces on top of the two trunks. Once the gaps were filled in with earth, so the feet of the oxen would not poke through, the road would be ready for use again. Eight dead oxen and a lot of charred timbers lay at the sides.

"We can use a brace of my animals to haul these critters away into the trees," the bullpuncher said.

"Tomorrow," Raider said.

"My animals ain't doing nothing while we're stuck here," the bullpuncher argued. "Tomorrow it will be a waste of working time. And some of the crazy bulls ain't going to pass these dead ones if they're left close by."

"Leave them," Raider said.

"What the hell for? The other two blowouts, the sons of bitches who blew the road came back after our boys had gone and ate part of the animals. You want to feed them, is that it? Oh, now I see." His crafty eyes glistened. "You're gonna lie in wait for them."

Raider said, "I'm heading back to Little River with the rest of the men here, once we've finished."

The bullpuncher looked longingly at his goad, as if he'd like to use it on some folk around here. He turned his back and headed toward his oxen around the bend.

"Silas, come help me burn up this charred wood without starting a forest fire," Raider said. "I don't want to leave any extra firewood lying around."

"How do you reckon they do it?" Silas asked as they worked.

"They bury the sticks of dynamite in the roadbed and know exactly how long the length of fuse will burn before it ignites the cap. They figure out how fast the bull team is moving, light the fuse when the oxen are a certain distance away, then run for cover."

"Bastards!" Silas growled. "It'd be cleaner just to shoot them."

"This is more frightening. How many men have quit this week after the two earlier blowouts?"

"Near on forty. Some old sourdoughs like that bullpuncher who was just here won't quit no matter what anyone throws at them. For them, it makes life interesting."

Raider grinned. "I kind of share that view."

"Hell, some folks go looking for trouble. I been running from it all my life, and it keeps on catching up with me."

They got the fire going good, consuming all the handy pieces of wood left over from the explosion. They added some of the newly sawed-off extra lengths discarded from the rebuilding of the road. While the final touches were being put to the road and the fire was dying down, a horseman approached from the west. He carefully drew out six sticks of dynamite from his saddlebags, for which Raider had earlier sent him back to Little River.

The workers cheered as the bull train and logs passed over the newly repaired section of skid road. They collected their tools and prepared to leave.

Raider couldn't handle an ax in the expert way these men could, so he showed Silas what he wanted done.

The two men waited until nearly dusk to ride back to where they had set off the charge.

"Forty dollars apiece for each team we blow. That makes it a hundred and twenty each in only one week. I've worked two months, seven days a week, sunup to sundown, for that kind of money. Another week of this and we're gonna be rich."

His partner grinned. "To hell with these lumber towns. We'll take the money down to the city and treat ourselves like kings. Maybe we'll put in a third week if Stanton needs us."

"He won't. If we keep this up, another three next week, there won't be a man jack left to haul the lumber from the logging camp to the sawmill. They're already quitting wholesale. This time next week, we'll be looking for a ship bound for San Francisco."

The other man whooped. "Until then we stay put in the woods. They'll be looking for us in the towns. The dumb bastards will never guess we're living off what we kill. I hope we get some young ox this time. That last lot was tough and stringy."

The two men spent a long time circling the site, searching for watchers and checking for ambushes. It was almost dark when they dismounted at the carcasses.

"You get a fire going while I butcher this here one."

As the flames built up, they used the firelight to prepare the meat and set up a spit.

"This meat ain't so bad. Throw some more logs on that fire."

His partner gathered two freshly sawed-off ends and approached the fire. As he came, part of one piece of wood fell away and a stick of dynamite fell on the ground. They could both see it plainly by the light of the fire. The man looked at the piece of wood in his hand and saw how a space had been hollowed out of it to hold the dynamite and how the bark had been pushed back on to hide it.

The men looked at one another for a terrified moment as the same thought occurred to them simultaneously. Then they looked at the fire. What about the wood they had already put on?

If they had started running even a few seconds earlier, they might have made it. They were running but they were still on their feet and not behind cover when the fire exploded outward in all directions. The wood had insulated the dynamite stick from the flames until the heat became too intense and triggered the explosion. The first blast set off a second stick, in another log on the fire, which gave the explosion a slightly delayed double impact.

A four-foot length of glowing timber, flying through the air with the speed of a swallow, hit one man square on the back. The impact of the heavy wood snapped his spine, and the embers set his clothes on fire as he lay on the ground with the timber half embedded in his body.

The second man was hit by only a few small pieces of wood. However, he was lifted off his feet and slammed to the forest floor by the double shock wave of the blast. He lay there winded, gasping for breath, while the undergrowth blazed around him. He was asphyxiated by smoke before the flames reached his flesh.

CHAPTER SIX

An early rider from the logging camp brought back the news about the two bodies and a fresh fire at the site of yesterday's blast. The flames were burning themselves out on this windless day on the logged-over area. Some more damage had been caused to the skid road through the burning of crosspieces. Cal Blair dispatched a crew of men, along with a sheriff's deputy, to clear things up.

"Reckon they were setting something else up and it went off in their faces," Cal said to the deputy.

"Good riddance," the lawman said.

Cal, Raider, and everyone else saw no reason to complicate the deputy's job by remembering any details which might not agree with this conclusion.

After they had gone, Raider asked Cal, "You think they brought the dynamite up from San Francisco or bought it local?"

"No schooner captain will carry it on his ship. They

had to get it here. And the only place to get it is at the
Excelsior Powder Works, which used to be in Mendocino City until one Sunday morning, no one there, the
place blew. Spontaneous combustion. Mendocino
wouldn't let them rebuild inside the city limits, so now
the place is halfway between Little River and there. It's
on a branch off the main trail, a few hundred yards in.
You can't see it from the trail, but most everyone knows
where it is. What have you in mind?"

"Maybe I'll have a chance to tie Stanton to the dynamite," Raider said.

"Even if he did buy some, that won't prove anything," Cal objected. "Everyone uses dynamite here—
to move rocks, tree stumps, dig holes."

"Stanton don't do that kind of work. If Stanton
bought some, it might not stand up as evidence against
him in a court of law, but you and me know why he
bought it."

"We sure do."

"That's all I need to know," Raider said. "It's time I
had a face-to-face talk with Stanton. I hear he's been
avoiding me—he walks the other way real fast when
I'm coming his way. So I been told, though to my
knowledge I've never set eyes on him. Up till now,
there's been nothing I could pin on him—or even accuse him of. I'm hoping for a connection here, since
dynamite ain't something you want to travel with if you
can buy it near where you intend to use it. I'll leave
Trotter here and take Silas with me."

"Do you think they might attack the mill with dynamite?" Cal asked.

"Why break up the thing he wants. It's us that Stanton wants destroyed, not the sawmill."

Raider and Silas Hanks rode out to the Excelsior Powder Works, which was a collection of shacks among rotting tree stumps. They could see two men at work through the open door of the largest shack. Water from a brook running just above the shack came through a pipe and entered a wooden trough in the middle of the floor. The trough emptied out the other end through another pipe which ran through a wall and ended close by, creating a large muddy pool. Ten five-gallon crocks stood half submerged in the trough, and next to each one stood a much smaller crock. One of the men passed along the line of crocks, adding a little from the small crock to its larger neighbor, stirring the contents with a stick, then passing on to the next one. When he finished the line of crocks, he went back to the first one again, repeating the procedure. The second man was stirring a large tub of liquid with a wooden paddle. Both of them ignored Raider and Silas.

Raider, who knew something about explosives, backed away and brought Silas with him by the arm. "That's not the way I'd care to make nitroglycerin," he said. "Do you ever see in the newspapers about those nitrating houses that blow up and leave no trace of the people that were in it. That's what you're looking at now."

Silas needed no further persuading to move back. "What's in those crocks?"

"The big ones hold nitric acid and the small ones glycerin. After adding a little glycerin to the acid, he gives each crock a chance to cool for a while in the water before adding more glycerin to the nitric acid. Neither one is explosive by itself, but put them together and you've got nitroglycerin. That liquid can mean a lot of trouble if a spark or a shock or even a sudden temperature change causes it to blow. It's what miners call blasting oil."

"Yeah, I've seen it used," Silas said, "instead of black powder."

"Nitroglycerin is much more powerful, but it's more dangerous to handle. Sometimes it just blows and no one knows what set it off. Most times there ain't much left to tell the story."

Silas looked in the open door at the two men working. "You think the folk in Mendocino City had the right idea in getting rid of them out here? What's in that tub he's stirring?"

"When the crocks are mixed, they pour them into a tub of water to dilute the nitroglycerin a bit. That's right—that's nitroglycerin he's swilling around in that tub. If that blows, it'll send his belt buckle to the moon."

"Us too."

"Maybe partway."

Silas and Raider retreated some more while they waited for the men to finish the batch of nitroglycerin in the crocks. The two men emptied the tub into canisters, then added water. One emptied the crocks while the other stirred. Silas held his breath while he watched. When he had finished, the one who had emptied the crocks came out to meet them, leaving the other man to wield the wooden paddle.

Raider showed him his Pinkerton identification. "Got a question for you. You sell dynamite lately to a man named Stanton?"

"I don't recall," the man said. He was small, with a

big gut that hung out over his belt and a protruding
lower lip that gave him a stubborn expression.

"I see," Raider said politely, putting away his identification papers. "Mind if I ask whether you own this
place or only work here?"

"I own it, lock, stock, and barrel. Anything that gets
sold, I sell it." His snarling, truculent voice made it
clear he intended to answer no more questions.

"Well, I'm here to look out for the Eagle Timber
Company," Raider told him. "You may have heard your
dynamite's being used to kill men and cause damage."

"Ain't my dynamite."

"I'm pretty sure it is," Raider said. "There's nowhere
else around to buy the stuff. You know what I was
thinking? That if your place wasn't around any longer
—you know, suppose you had a big accident—then
maybe the folks at Eagle wouldn't have to worry about
getting their asses blown off by your product."

"That's hard talk, mister." He stared at Raider eyeball to eyeball and did not back off an inch.

"I'm glad you understand me," Raider said very
quietly.

A muscle in the man's cheek twitched. Then again.
He couldn't control it. He started to talk, fast and urgently. "I had nothing to do with them attacks, mister. I
just make the stuff, and I don't ask no questions. You
can't blame me. I had nothing to do with it."

"Not then, you didn't," Raider said. "I believe that.
It's only now you're involving yourself."

"How?"

"Holding back information." Raider let that sink in.
"I'm not asking you to stand before some judge and
hold a Bible in your hand. I'm not even asking you to

face someone and point your finger. I just want an answer to a single question. Have you sold dynamite to Stanton in the last few weeks?"

"About ten days ago."

"How much?"

"A hundred sticks."

"To Stanton himself?"

"To him and two fellas who was with him."

Raider slapped him on the back. "That's what I needed to know. You have a half dozen sticks to sell me?"

"What do you want them for?"

"I thought you never asked questions."

"I don't. I just don't want you to use them on me."

"Don't worry abut that," Raider assured him. "All you have to do to stay friends with me is, next time Stanton buys, you send someone to let me know."

"Sure thing. Come on over here to the mixing house. I have some fresh sticks made yesterday. Top-grade. Unless you want me to mix you some new dynamite. I have the rottenstone here. Three parts of that to one part of nitroglycerin—ain't no secret in that. Trick is in the mixing."

"We been reading in the newspaper about nitrating houses and mixing houses," Silas said. "Don't you go mixing that shit while I'm in here. I don't know why people couldn't stay with black powder anyhow."

"I'll tell you why," the dynamite man said. "That old black powder is a mixture of sulphur, carbon, and salt-peter. It goes off with a big bang and a lot of smoke, but it don't pack much punch. Not against stone, anyway. Then blasting oil came along. That packed punch but was a bitch to handle, and you could only put it in vertical boreholes because it was a liquid. Then someone in Europe thought up the idea of mixing the blasting oil with stuff like potter's clay, which would make it safer to handle. Once they been made up, you can cut my sticks of dynamite with a knife. Want me to show you something?"

He went into the mixing house and came back out, holding one stick of dynamite. He lit a match and held it under the stick, so that the flame touched the material. Silas was ready to dive for cover behind a nearby tree stump, but he stood his ground because Raider didn't flinch and because it was clear the man holding the dynamite was testing their nerve. Silas felt his mouth go dry.

When the match burnt out, Raider said, "I'll need some blasting caps and a length of quick fuse." He spoke casually, like he wished the dynamite man would quit fooling around, wasting their time.

"Quick fuse?"

"You heard me."

He went back into the mixing house and this time came back with six sticks, six blasting caps, and a length of fuse. "You won't need no spare blasting caps," he said, holding one up, a short metal tube about the diameter of a .38 bullet. "These is guaranteed to work. Latest kind. You have three different grades of explosive in here. The fuse sets off the ignition compound, which sets off the priming charge, and that in turn sets off the base charge. The base charge sets off your dynamite—and up she goes."

Silas Hanks pointed out Stanton to Raider. Stanton was seated on a high stool at a counter just inside the door of his warehouse, near the Mendocino City wharves. On the counter in front of him were a big ledger book, some pens and an inkwell, an ink blotter, and a Peacemaker .45. Stanton saw Raider coming too late. He had nowhere to run.

Raider and Silas walked into the warehouse, which was weathered and decrepit, obviously constructed in a hurry a couple of decades ago from whatever logs had little or no commercial value. The building stood alone, surrounded by vacant space.

Stanton made no move for his gun, instead bracing himself for a yelling match with the big Pinkerton. Raider said not one word to him. He walked in with Silas, stopped in front of the counter, pulled out a stick of dynamite from a burlap bag, and forced a blasting cap into one end.

"Put it over there," he said to Silas, pointing toward a huge pile of crates.

Stanton was a cool customer. He didn't react. He just sat there and let Raider have Silas plant all six sticks in his merchandise stacks.

Raider pulled out the length of fuse, saying to Silas, "Go outside. Keep people away."

He worked on connecting the fuse to each of the six blasting caps. He needed both hands for the work, and his Remington was in its holster. Stanton had his Peacemaker on the counter next to his right hand. Raider could only watch him out of the corner of his eye, needing to look carefully at what he was doing in connecting the fuse. It seemed a reasonable match. No one could blame Stanton for killing a rogue Pinkerton who tried to blow up his warehouse. Stanton was sorely tempted. He might have taken up the challenge if he thought the circumstances were accidental, but this challenge was being offered to him on a plate. That goddamn Pinkerton wanted him to reach for that Peacemaker inches away from his hand. In fact, the Pinkerton was betting he couldn't resist going for his weapon to save his warehouse. It was all a bluff. Once he went for the gun, the Pinkerton would be justified in shooting him. And this man was nothing but a trained professional killer. Stanton wouldn't have a chance.

Would the Pinkerton blow up his warehouse? Probably not. This was all a ruse to goad him into going for his gun. Well, Stanton had an answer for that. He would sit on his stool at the counter and outwait and outstare this fool who thought he could panic him.

Raider was busy doing a last-minute check on connections, then unreeled the fuse as he backed toward the open door. He went right out the door, unreeling as he went, and disappeared from Stanton's view.

Stanton waited, a smile on his face. He knew the Pinkerton would have to find some pretext to come back inside. Then he would have lost, and Stanton won. He heard a hissing noise and looked down. The fuse was burning! He could see its burning point moving rapidly across the floor like an insect, leaving a trail of ash in its wake. Too late now to stamp it out or pull the unburned fuse loose from the dynamite sticks. He'd be lucky if he made it out the door.

Stanton ran so fast he left his gun behind. Raider and Silas, hunkered down behind a stack of lumber, saw him come out the door like a prairie dog from a hole with a ferret on its tail. He ran a few paces and flung himself face down on the ground.

The first blast set off one or two other sticks even

before the burning fuse reached them. Then there was a pause for a few seconds before the remaining sticks all blew more or less together. The roof sank into the building on the first explosion, the windows blew outward, and the log wall they could see shook but held firm. The second explosion knocked some of the lower logs out of this wall, and those above came tumbling down and rolled loose. There were no belching flames, and not much smoke. It was only when pieces of packing cases began to rain down on the them that they realized much of the merchandise had been blown sky high.

Stanton jumped to his feet, dusty and disheveled, and ran toward the wharves.

Stanton made it to Manchester before sundown in his sailboat. He expected Jeff Dench's scowl on seeing him, and he got one. Dench paid well, and he expected people to do his bidding without bothering him with complications. To hell with Dench.

"If you can find someone better than me to do your dirty work, go ahead and hire him." These were Stanton's first words. "If you can't, you better listen to what I have to say and listen real good, because you have a problem as well as me. It's that Pinkerton, Raider. Everything I throw at him, he swats it like it's only a fly. You won't believe this. Today he walked into my warehouse and dynamited it. You got to make good on my loss, Mr. Dench. This ain't fair. I'm getting hurt."

Dench said nothing for a moment. "I'll pay. That's nothing to me, Stanton. What gets to me is I ain't never seen you like this before. You been shook."

"I sure have, and I'm telling you, Mr. Dench, you

don't deal with this Pinkerton fast and you'll be shook too."

"You can't handle him on your own?"

"No, sir."

"I never thought I'd live to see the day when I have to listen to that from you, Stanton."

"I told you, Mr. Dench, there's only one man I'd back against that Pinkerton son of a bitch and that's One-Ear Draper. Even he got scared off. Now, I could go on down to San Francisco and hire us some real scum, fast and trigger-happy. They'd get rid of Raider for you, but doing it that open would surely set all of Little River and Mendocino City against you when it came time for you to take over. Folks up that way will tolerate only so much. They're liable to do anything if we don't act careful. But I'm running scared, Mr. Dench, and I don't mind telling you that between us, though I wouldn't want no one else to hear it. You want for me to bring in a shipload of badmen from the city? Say the word."

"No. I intend to walk careful in these parts. I appreciate your honesty and good judgment, Stanton, in admitting to me you can't handle Raider. My people have been checking into him. Seems he's famous in cow country, all the way from Canada down to Mexico. He don't come this far west all that often, which accounts for how he could ship in unbeknownst to us and cut up our men. You spotted him. Your judgment's good."

"I figured he'd done a lot of harm in other places," Stanton said, soothed by the compliments.

"Also, your advice on not bringing in an army is good. Them state-of-Mainers is a funny crowd, and they control all the logging on this coast. Set them against you and you won't find a man willing to fell a tree. I been through it here in Manchester, and I don't want to set them against me up in Little River. You know where to find One-Ear?"

"I think so," Stanton said.

"If he was to kill Raider, it would be seen as a blood feud between the two. Not even the Pinkerton Agency could pin it on us. Find him, Stanton. Offer him gold. Give him coin to hire sidekicks. Then leak word out where he can be found."

"Raider will go after him."

The two men smiled, pleased at this prospect.

Raider knew he had made an awful mistake. There was nothing for it now but to stick it out and thank the Lord when he escaped. He was trapped. His eyes darted left and right, but he saw no way out. He was sitting in a soft armchair in the widow Blair's drawing room, trying to hold sandwiches hardly bigger than his fingernail and drink tea out of a cup fragile as an eggshell. He couldn't think of anything to say, was afraid to relax in case he'd break something, and couldn't figure out why he should be willing to go through this in the hope of getting laid, when all he had to do was walk in any saloon in Little River or Mendocino City and take his pick. It made no sense. If he was lying in some water-logged ditch or balanced on a tree limb high above the ground, waiting in ambush for some law-breaking varmint, he'd feel a lot more comfortable than he was now, in this upholstered chair, holding bits of bread you'd feed to a canary bird and drinking bear-piss tea.

Brenda was chattering on about the town library, which Raider pretended to be familiar with until she explained that there wasn't one in Little River and she was trying to get one started. He was thinking about suddenly standing up, dropping everything, and making a bolt for the door when Brenda suddenly subsided in gales of laughter.

Raider looked at her suspiciously. Nothing funny had been said. Was this hysterics? After all, she had only recently lost her husband. Maybe he should go. Right at this moment.

"You ever seen an unbroken colt locked into a stable?" she asked him, trying to stifle her laughter. "Raider, I swear that's what you look like right now. You want to smoke? Smoke. No, you don't smoke. You want a drink. I'll get you a bottle. Kick off your boots, man. Let me hear what you have to say."

It took some time for her to persuade Raider she had not gone off the deep end.

"Just because you didn't find me guzzling gin in some dive with red wallpaper, my face painted, and a good piece of one leg showing under a French gown doesn't mean I ain't a willing woman, Raider."

Raider still didn't know what to say, but he had a fair idea of what to do. He caressed and comforted her, kissed her lips and neck, fondled her body through her dress. When he lifted her up in his arms, she pointed toward the staircase.

On the bed, he kissed her some more, fondled her body, and removed her clothes, piece by piece. He sucked on her creamy smooth tits and rolled each nipple between his tongue and the roof of his mouth. Her nipples were hard and swollen, standing out from her breasts.

As his hand glided down over her stomach, he felt

her body writhe and then tense as his fingers reached her fuzz. Her clit peeped out at him from her juicy slit. His fingertip teased the erectile nub of her clit, and he could feel her whole body shaking as violent waves of ecstasy coursed through her.

Raider licked her breasts and her neck. He sucked some more on her tits, all the time exciting her further between the legs. He drove his tongue deep into her mouth.

Two fingers slid into the moist recess of her sex. He worked them back and forth inside her until her body seethed under his touch.

Then he mounted her and sank his shaft into her hungry depths. He hammered his rod into her until she climaxed in a series of little yelps, finishing with one long howl that would have made any wolf proud.

CHAPTER SEVEN

Cal Blair came in one morning with word that One-Ear Draper was at Rockport, a sawmill town about thirty miles up the coast. He had killed a man in a fair fight outside a saloon. He was calling himself by some other name than Eugene Draper, but sure as this man had only one nose, he had only one ear.

"Sure sounds like him," Raider said. "I thought he'd probably cleared out of this area. But now he's still around, Cal, you can depend on it that sooner or later Stanton will hire him again to hassle you."

"I know it."

"Trotter, you take care of things here. You and Cal stay at the sawmill. If there's trouble inland, send in Silas Hanks with some good men. Don't you or Cal go yourselves. We always got to think this may be a diversion to lure me away so they can hit while I'm gone."

"I was thinking that," Trotter said.

Raider believed it. Samuel Trotter lived only to be a Pinkerton. His mind was always buzzing over something, like a trapped wasp. Playing chess for him was a form of light relaxation after a bout of serious thinking. This kind of Pinkerton was wasted here in the redwoods. He should be catching crooks on Wall Street or in Washington, D.C. No one could outthink a man like One-Ear Draper, because One-Ear did not think. Trotter might have a lot of smart maneuvers in chess, but he had to suppose his opponent was playing to the same set of rules that he was. One-Ear had no rules. He wasn't playing any game. He was down there with the animals —eat or be eaten, kill or be killed. A thinking man was liable not to realize what he was up against.

Raider was still wary that Trotter might have been sent to spy on him—even unintentionally on Trotter's part. An innocent, green operative with a big mouth can blab about a lot of things in his reports without meaning harm to anyone. Trotter of course had heard about Stanton's warehouse, and Raider had to tell him not to mention it in any of his reports to Chicago. "Don't believe what these fellas tell you. You don't want to go spreading stories like that about me."

"But I do believe them," Trotter said.

"Heresay evidence," Raider scoffed. "You'd be assassinating the reputation of a fellow Pinkerton if you put gossip like that down on paper."

"Are you saying you didn't blow up Stanton's warehouse?" Trotter inquired, reasonably enough.

"Don't you question me. Just be damn sure you don't make insulting remarks about me in any of your damn-fool reports."

It had taken a while, but Samuel Trotter was beginning to get the message. He had heard about Raider since his first week in training as a Pinkerton. He had even met occasional operatives who boasted of having once worked with him on a job, although his usual partner had been the famous Doc Weatherbee, who was retired now from the agency. Raider broke all the regulations because he was Raider. Trotter himself liked regulations and always tried to observe them. Yet he couldn't help admiring Raider for not caring about them. He would see that Raider could hold no tale-telling grudge against him. It was all right to tell stories about Raider—so long as they didn't become part of official reports.

Trotter now saw why Raider had been avoiding him. "I'm not watching over your shoulder and writing down what you do," he told Raider earnestly. "Hey, I'm more afraid of what you might tell Chicago about me."

Raider laughed. "If I complained about you, kid, Chicago would take it as a compliment to you. If I say I like you, then they know they can't trust you."

"I'm not selling my soul to Chicago."

"Glad to hear it," Raider said.

After he'd made the arrangements with Trotter about looking after the Eagle Timber Company while he was gone, Raider had Silas Hanks and three other men row him in a longboat offshore until they were in the path of schooners traveling north.

Silas and the men knew most of the captains, and they shouted to passing ships until they found one headed for Rockport. The wind was light, and the schooner was moving slowly. They brought the longboat alongside, and crewmen on the schooner deck threw down a rope ladder. Raider jumped onto the ladder and seconds later found himself dangling over open water as the two vessels parted company. He made a less than graceful ascent onto the deck on the swaying rope ladder, nearly losing his treasured black Stetson. When he stepped onto the deck, one crewman yelled, "Ahoy, cowboy!"

"There's a lot of things you can say against a horse and against the prairie," Raider answered him. "But at least when you fall off one onto the other, you don't drown or get et by a shark."

On the way north, the ship stayed close to shore and passed the timber-loading coves of Mendocino City, Caspar, Noyo, Fort Bragg, Inglewood, Kibesillah, Westport, and Usal before coming to Rockport just before sundown. The schooner anchored offshore, since loading could not begin until daylight the next day. However, the crew saw no reason to waste time bobbing up and down at anchor when they could be ashore raising some hell. Raider went with the first boatload of men.

Rockport was nothing but a collection of bleak, weather-beaten shacks, without any proper street or just about anything else. The nearest woman was eleven and a half miles away, down in Westport, a journey by boat. Two of the shacks sold liquor and had card tables. The liquor was bad and the cards were marked. In a place like this, there was going to be no place for Draper to hide. There wasn't much else to be said for Rockport.

Neither was Raider hard for Draper's men to find. He was plainly not a seaman and not a lumberjack, and so attracted attention when he set foot in Rockport. Stanton had told Draper to stay put, hire some guns, and let

Raider come to him. Draper told him there were no guns for hire in Rockport, so Stanton sent him three men. Stanton leaked the word where Draper might be found, and One-Ear and the three hirelings watched and waited. They had hired on at the sawmill, splitting logs, and all four men saw Raider arrive with some of the crewmen on a small boat from the schooner. There were only a few places he could sleep that night, and only two saloons where he could drink.

The so-called saloons were good-sized shacks made of reject boards from the sawmill. The bar consisted of two long, heavy boards on top of two big barrels. Only whiskey, gin, and brandy were served, all from five-gallon crocks. The felt-covered card tables and the chairs around them had seen long use before they came to Rockport to end their days.

One-Ear winked at the others when they saw Raider get out of the boat. He told them to stay on the job. There was nowhere for Raider to go. They had him where they wanted him. Now all they had to do was handle him carefully.

When they quit work at the mill, One-Ear hid out in a friend's shack, in case Raider had already discovered the cabin the four men were sharing. The other three walked the town in search of the Pinkerton. One spotted him in the saloon outside of which Draper had killed a man days previously. He collected the other two, and they set out to do things the way Draper had told them.

When the three walked into the crowded saloon, Raider had no way of knowing them. Like most of the men there, they did not carry firearms—only foot-long hunting knives with a honed blade that could sever a rope in a single swipe, a necessity on the job of maneuvering big redwood logs. They didn't pick on Raider, directing their remarks instead at the seaman he was drinking with. The men off the schooner took the first remarks as jokes, and they in turn made some comments about lumberjacks. This was taken personally by some other woodsmen in the place, and the talk soon expanded into unfavorable comparisons of Norway and the state of Maine. This naturally resulted in some personal remarks and some speculation about the parentage of individuals present.

The seafarers struck the first blows, and the treefellers responded in kind. It was mostly fists and boots, without recourse to knives. Raider pulled back against a wall, moving as far out of the way of the fight as he could. When one lumberjack approached, the Pinkerton floored him with an uppercut. The woodsman staggered to his feet again, then took another punch in the head, this time from a Norwegian seaman. He decided to stay down after that.

Next Raider was jumped by three woodsmen. He hammered at them with his fists, not connecting hard enough to bring any of them down but, all the same, making it clear that he could more than hold his own, back to the wall, against all three of them.

While two of them struck at him and took the blows he showered on them, the third used them as cover in order to try to move in close to the Pinkerton. Raider knew the tactic and thought the man had a gun. He didn't want to chance using his own revolver in this crowded space, in what he still saw as a drunken pitched battle rather than as a meaningful fight. In a surprise change from his defensive posture, he charged his two attackers, breaking between them through to the man behind them.

The third man was holding his knife blade down out of sight, next to his right leg. That was the arm Raider went for. The man tried to hook the blade up into Raider's belly, but the Pinkerton's left hand had already clamped above his elbow, pinioning that arm against his body. Raider used his right hand to push him in the chest, knocking him off balance and onto his back on the floor, among the feet of the fighting men.

He was still holding his knife, looking up at the Pinkerton with blazing eyes. Raider remembered he had two more somewhere behind him, and lost no time. As the man tried to rise from the floor, Raider booted him across the forehead, flattening him again. Then he brought his right foot up and stomped down with all his force on the forearm of the hand holding the knife. He heard and felt the two bones crack under his boot.

The scream of pain the man let loose brought the fighting to a stop, as everyone looked down at him. The middle of his forearm now twisted off at an odd angle, and a snapped bone jutted through the broken skin. The man went on howling and flopping about like a seal out of water.

His two pards had their blades unsheathed, but for the moment they also stood and stared at the mutilated limb, spooked by the screaming. Little things like that didn't paralyze Raider. He kicked the nearest of the two men in the nuts, causing him to drop his knife, double up, and start howling as well, so it was like the monkey house in the zoo.

Raider scooped the knife up off the floor and held it out in front of him in time to ward off the attack of the third man. The other customers in the saloon had been so totally distracted by the knife-wielding combatants they had forgotten all about their own fistfights. Norwegians and state-of-Mainers, seamen and lumberjacks now stood shoulder to shoulder and made way for the two men cautiously circling each other with steel blades at the ready. The man with the horribly broken arm was ignored where he lay. There was nothing anybody enjoyed so much as a good knife fight.

Raider sized up his opponent as a good fighter. By now he had figured that these three men had been set on him by Draper. He had seen them start the insults that led to the saloon fight, and he guessed they had hoped to stab him in the confusion. There was no sign of One-Ear in the place. Probing and feinting, Raider estimated that he had two or three inches advantage in arm length, so he changed his tactics from cautious stalking, with the blade held flat for a thrust to the ribs, to punching wildly with the foot-long blade. He darted the knife point indiscriminately at whatever he could—chest, eye, hand, shoulder.

He started to connect in the upper chest and upper arms—just small stabs of less than an inch of steel into the flesh, before his opponent pulled back. But these jabs were enough to break the skin, draw blood, and cause pain. The blood and pain caused more confusion than weakness in the man. Each jab made the crowd roar with approval. Men were shouting odds and taking bets. Raider backed him off relentlessly, round and round in the clearing made by the men, punishing him methodically.

The man knew he was the loser. He had nowhere to go. Raider was too close to him at all times for him to turn his back and try to break through the circle of men. They would not willingly let him escape. The big Pinkerton was so sure of himself, he never bothered with the six-gun on his hip. The man saw it as his only chance—he had to lay his hands on that revolver.

Dropping his knife, he ran in under Raider's blade to grab the Remington out of its holster. Raider plunged the knife tip into the muscle of his upper left arm and pushed hard until he felt the blade scrape against the bone.

The man clutched at his arm with his right hand, all thought of grabbing the gun driven from his mind by the searing pain. He sank to his knees, his mouth clamped shut and his eyes rolling in his head.

Raider jerked the blade out of his muscle and twisted the fingers of his left hand in the man's long oily black hair. He yanked back on the man's head and cut a few inches along the top of the forehead, at the hairline.

As the honed blade edge parted the skin in a bright red line, Raider bellowed, "I'm gonna hang this scalp on that wall yonder and buy y'all a drink."

This drew a big cheer. Then the men quieted down so they could enjoy the details of the scalping.

The man's eyes were glazed with fear, and he looked up at Raider with dread.

Raider said to him, "Unless you'd prefer me to cut off your ear."

"Paxton," the man gasped, with a shred of hope in his voice. "Paxton sent us."

"Who the hell's Paxton?"

"Joe Paxton. Like you said, he has only one ear."

Raider lifted the blade from his forehead. Blood

welled from a line about four inches long and ran down into one of his eyes.

"Help your pard over there," the Pinkerton said. "Make a splint for his arm and go with him on the first ship out of here."

The man tried to kiss Raider's boot, and Raider got blood on the calfskin Middleton kicking his face away.

The one Raider had kicked in the balls recovered while his pard seemed about to lose his scalp. He snuck out of the saloon and went to warn Joe Paxton, the name by which he knew Draper.

"He's loco, Joe," the man said. "Way he is tonight, if he comes up here, he's gonna cut your other ear off."

Draper bristled at the reference to his missing ear. "Don't talk shit," he said. "The man's a Pinkerton. He can't do like you and I can."

"I just seen the varmint stomp arm bones. My last sight of him, he was lifting Billy's hair. Only I snuck away, God knows what he'd have done to me. All I know is I wouldn't be in fit condition to stand here before you if he'd caught me."

"You think he's gone loco?" Draper asked.

"Plumb crazy."

As someone who wavered on the line of sanity and madness frequently himself, Draper saw nothing unlikely or unusual in the Pinkerton's decline into irrationality and mayhem. "We ain't got nothing to do but run off into the woods in the dark or stand and fight him," he said.

"Run off into the woods," the other man chose without hesitation. "I'd have done it myself except I came by here to warn you."

"'Preciate that. You ought to know I been running from that dude for years. He comes after me sometimes in my nightmares. I'd sure sleep better knowing he was pushing up grass."

"You going to be the one pushing up grass, Joe."

"No way. Harry, he's going to be along here soon, looking for me. Looking for you, too. You and me know this, and that gives us a chance to get to him first."

Draper crossed the shack to the locked chest in which they stored their guns.

Raider knew one of the three men had left the saloon and presumably had gone to warn Draper. He was told how to find the cabin that the four men shared. Raider knew that One-Ear would be expecting him and could be depended on to give him a hot reception. The town of Rockport had no marshal. Except for the saloon and store owners, everybody there worked for the lumber company, and the company fired anyone who caused trouble. That was the extent of law enforcement. When Draper had killed a man outside one of the saloons, it had been judged a fair fight and he kept his job. Once a man had been brought down to Westport to stand trial, but usually they did their own hanging if the mob felt so inclined.

If Raider wanted to go after the man he called Draper and they knew as Paxton, that was all right with them. If Paxton killed Raider, in their view he had good cause to. If Raider killed him, that was fine too—so long as it was fair, with no back-shooting or other trickery. Needless to say, Raider found himself alone.

It was a clear night, still and very dark. What small

light the stars gave seemed to be absorbed by the big
evergreen trees all around. The shack the four men
shared was only five minutes' walk from the saloon, but
Raider could only just make out the outlines of things
and he had to go slowly. As he neared the end of town
where the shack was, he also went quietly. He would be
just as hard for Draper to see as Draper would be for
him. What Raider had to avoid was shooting some
townsman who just happened by.

One-Ear's shack was close by two others. Raider had
been told back in the saloon that he would know the
three shacks from the small horse corral opposite them
and a big outcrop of rock right next to the one lived in
by One-Ear. In some of the cabins along the way, kerosene lamps showed some signs of life. At this end of
town, not even a candle showed. The ground was un-
even, and he stumbled continually, making his approach
somewhat less than silent. He could see the shapes of
some cabins ahead, but no corral or rock outcrop. A
sensible man would have waited for daylight, but Raider
pressed on, knowing that waiting was a luxury he
couldn't afford when dealing with One-Ear.

Raider stumbled on through the darkness, getting
nearer to the outlines of the cabins. He hunkered down
low so his own outline would not be visible against the
stars, and he moved forward and away from the cabins
until he felt a corral rail. He slipped between the rails,
drew his revolver, and eased softly forward. A nearby
sound almost caused him to shoot in that direction, but
he recognized it soon enough to hold back—the stamp
of a hoof of a horse nervous at his closeness. Raider
hoped Draper and his pard, if they were within hearing

distance, would not register the significance of the sound.

He moved on until he was almost opposite the third cabin and saw the irregular outline of rock close to it. He was startled this time by the sudden restlessness of two horses, which moved to the far end of the corral from him in a clatter of hooves on the earth. Raider used the noise to slip out between the rails and cross toward the cabin. His toe touched a loose stone on the ground. This gave him an idea. Changing his gun to his left hand, he picked up the stone and chucked it through the window of Draper's cabin. Glass shattered.

A lamp was lit in the shack next door. Its glow momentarily revealed a crouching figure between the cabins. Gun back in his shooting hand, Raider blasted two shots at the figure. At the sound of the shots, the lamp was extinguished and all was dark again.

Raider changed his position fast, knowing that his weapon's muzzle flashes had revealed his location. He couldn't tell if either of his shots had hit home. Lamps were being lit in more distant cabins, but the next-door neighbor apparently intended to throw no more light on the subject.

Suddenly, from a point on Raider's left, flame spat and six rapid shots rang out. None of the bullets came close to him, so the gunman was firing at the place where he had been. Raider snapped off four quick shots at the spot where the muzzle flashes were. Then he had to move fast and reload his gun.

He saw or heard nothing more. It was twenty minutes before men with rifles and lamps came to check the scene. Raider called to them and had them look where the gunman had shot at him. Seemingly none of his four

bullets had found their mark. Then he had them look in
the space between the two shacks, where he had seen
the figure crouching.

A man lay there on his back, two spreading blotches
of red on his white shirtfront, his eyes open, a Colt still
clutched in his right hand.

Someone who had been in the saloon said to Raider,
"That's the fella you toed in the balls a while back."

Raider said sadly, "It's been a rough night for him."

"He ain't in the town, he ain't on the water, so
there's only one other place he can be—in the woods,"
the sawmill foreman told Raider. "That Paxton ain't got
no comrades in Rockport, save the three you know
about. Some folk would've liked to have done something about that killing he did, but they was afraid of
him. Sure as hell, no one's going to hide him or give
him help—'cept at gunpoint. Now, we been through
every building in this town, and there ain't nothing else.
You can track him real easy if he goes up or down the
coast, but I know where he's gone: that boy's headed
inland. He'll follow one of the logging trails in after he
stole a horse, buy himself a grubstake at the logging
camp, and cross the mountains due east. He'll have to
let the horse free and go on foot. But t'other side of the
mountains, you have cattle and ranch country. He can
lose himself—and you—real easy there."

"How many logging camps are in the woods back of
here?" Raider asked.

"Just the one."

"Let me hire a horse. I'll leave it at the camp."

"You can take one free, and I can send a man with
you to show you the way. But you better sit down first

and have a big breakfast. You mightn't see a plate of good fried food again for several days."

When Raider and the man approached the logging camp, they found that Draper had been there and gone. No one at the camp had yet heard of any trouble in Rockport, so they had given him food and wished him luck on what he claimed was a gold-prospecting trip. While Raider was still at the camp, Draper's horse wandered in riderless. One logger who had done some winter trapping in the area explained to Raider the route he should take through the mountains. Draper would have to go more or less the same way; though he wouldn't necessarily always be restricted to just one stream valley, he wouldn't find many such gaps leading from west to east in these mountains that ran north to south.

Raider stocked up on food himself, went as far into the timbered hills as a horse could manage, then turned him over to the lumberman and continued on his own on foot. He kept moving throughout the day, pausing only once for a short while to eat and rest. Draper would be in a hurry to put as many miles as he could between him and the lumbering camps. He knew the woodsmen knew the forests better than he did and had to consider that some might be following him. As the sun got lower in the sky, Raider eased up. He guessed he hadn't traveled all that far, considering the effort he had put into it. Most of his energy had been burned up through pushing undergrowth aside and climbing up steep slopes. He was still in the foothills, with all the real mountains ahead. If he could end the chase today, he would save himself a lot of toil and hardship.

At the head of a wilderness valley, where he had a

view across a vast sweep of trees, he sat and watched. This was as good a place as any. He would spend the night here if he saw nothing. A cool evening breeze started, and that pleased him. Draper might build himself a fire to stay warm. He should be hungry, too. Some warm cooked food would sit well in his belly.

The Pinkerton was fairly sure that his quarry was somewhere in this valley, unless he had passed him and left him behind. Raider looked out over the treetops for a telltale wisp of smoke. There was nothing. The sun was getting very low. He figured there was less than an hour of daylight left. If Draper was smart, he would wait until dark before lighting his fire, so the column of smoke could not be seen. Finally, the sun set and Raider shivered with cold. His belly was empty and his mood sour. He was not looking forward to another day of pushing his way through pathless forests and hills. He collected wood for his own fire before darkness fell, deciding to wait a couple of hours before lighting it in order to make sure he was outlasting Draper in caution. While he waited in the darkness, cold and hungry, thinking ugly thoughts about One-Ear Draper, a sweet smell came to his nostrils—wood smoke!

Raider bounded to his feet and walked into the darkness toward where the smell seemed strongest. He moved as quietly as he could, though it was impossible for him to move silently because he could not see every twig that might snap and leaves that might rustle. He kept moving cautiously until he spotted the flames of the fire through the underbrush. Then he began to stalk in earnest.

With the fire to zero in on, he made good progress. He saw a figure outlined against the flames, throwing more wood on and turning meat on a spit, which he could now smell cooking. One-Ear was having himself a regular celebration!

Then he heard voices. Was Draper talking to himself? He had been alone at the logging camp. Who could he have met out here? Raider crept forward to investigate.

As he moved, he felt a sharp point, like a large thorn, poking him in the side. He looked down and saw a knife blade glint in the light from the fire. A moment later, a second blade was pressed against his throat from the other side. He felt his Remington being pulled from its holster. Then he was propelled forward with a slow careful shove, the two knives scratching at his skin. He still hadn't seen who had waylaid him.

They were pushing him toward the fire. When he reached it he saw three Indian warriors sitting around it, one casually turning a deer haunch on the spit. One of them glanced at him briefly, then pointed at a place on the ground near the fire. The two knives were withdrawn from their resting places in his side and throat.

Raider didn't need a second invitation to sit himself down.

For a while, Raider thought there were five Indians —the three around the fire and the two who had caught him by surprise. Gradually another six gathered around the fire, appearing in ones and twos from the darkness, so that there were eleven altogether. When Raider explained to the only one who spoke good English that he had not been attacking them, that he had been hunting down another white man wanted for crimes against his own people, this man urgently translated what he had said for the other and seven of them slipped away into the darkness again.

They told Raider they were Pomos from Round Valley, to the north of where they were tonight. They had been the most powerful group in this region before the white men brought cattle and cleared forest lands. Their people had been massacred in the fifties and sixties when they fought back to keep their ancestral lands. Now they were weak, powerless, confined to a reservation at Round Valley.

Raider tactfully didn't ask what they were doing down here. He suspected it might be for some religious purpose—and knew it would be safer for him to seem unaware of that. He wasn't quite sure what their real attitude was to him. Considering that they had caught him sneaking up on them, they were treating him very civilly. He had to admit he himself wouldn't have been half as friendly to a Pomo he had caught creeping up on his camp fire. But Raider knew enough not to be deceived by first appearances. In fact, he was kind of worried about these warriors being just too nice to him —especially when they insisted that he share their food with them. He responded by insisting that they share his also. This left him with no stores for the next day—but the way things were going, he couldn't be sure he was ever going to see another day.

They had almost finished eating when four Indians came in with Draper. He was looking plenty scared in the firelight until he set eyes on Raider. When he saw they had the Pinkerton, too, that cheered him up a bit. The Pomos fed Draper, and after they all had finished eating, they wanted to know what evil things One-Ear had done against his people. Raider recited a long list of his crimes. He would have liked to have told them that he must have done something to the Comanches, because they were the ones who cut off one of his ears— but he decided not to, in case that gave the Pomos any ideas.

Draper did not interrupt while Raider was talking and waited until everything had been translated. At that point, he waved his hat at the Pinkerton, called him a liar, and that he was a hired killer come to hunt him down and steal his wife.

Raider was somewhat upset that the Indians seemed to give equal weight to this story as to his own. Then he saw the game they were playing. This was all right with him. Draper hadn't seen it yet—he would be in for a surprise. One-Ear, warm, his belly full, with a circle of willing listeners, was holding forth on some bullshit about his imaginary wife and peaceful home that the gunslinger on the other side of the fire had broken up.

Raider let him talk. When One-Ear had used up his imagination, Raider kept it simple, saying exactly what he knew the Indians wanted to hear. He called Draper a liar, a killer, claimed to be insulted to such an extent that no apology could ever be enough to make up for it.

One-Ear still didn't get it. He blabbed on some more about Raider's attacks on his gentle wife and happy home. Raider once more called him a liar. The Indians nodded to one another, and one held up his hand for silence while he spoke. Raider knew what was going to come.

The Pomo who spoke English said that only one honorable way existed for the two white men to solve their differences. One must kill the other. The victor would be given back his gun and released the next morning.

They would get to keep the dead man's gun. Either way, the Pomos came out ahead.

One-Ear started stammering a long explanation, but the Pomo who understood English refused to listen to him. The Indians had their evening's entertainment fully arranged—a duel to the death between two of their oppressors. This suited Raider's plans just fine. It was Draper who hadn't seen it coming. This was just what he had been running from. He was trapped now. He was more of a prisoner in the forest with these Pomos than he would have been in any of the coastal logging towns. There at least he could have tried running. Here he had to stand and fight. There he might have had mercy from some believing soul. Here in the forest with embittered Pomo warriors and a mad-dog Pinkerton, there would be none.

Several of the Pomos were clearing a space next to the fire, while others where throwing fast-burning sticks into the flames, which blazed up and cast brighter light. Raider rose slowly to his feet, a lazy relaxed smile on his face. When Draper didn't move, the Indians still sitting around the fire gazed sternly at him until he too stood up.

"I'll need to check my gun," Raider said.

The Pomo translated this and was given a long speech in return. In response he went searching about on the ground and came back to the fireside with two heavy stones, one in each hand. He gave these to the warriors seated at the fire, and they passed them from one to the other, hefting them for weight and examining their sharp edges and points. While this was going on, Raider and One-Ear stood confronting one another, the Pinkerton patient and satisfied, the outlaw tense and trying to work himself into a murderous rage—not the easiest thing for a frightened man to do.

At last, the two stones having been approved, they were brought to the two white men by the English-speaking Pomo. "No guns. No knives. Just these stones only. Or things you pick up. One man lives. He sleeps. We feed him. We give him his gun. He goes in peace."

Even One-Ear could see by now that there was no room for discussion here, no point in arguing. The Pomo held up the stones between them, clearly expecting the fight to begin right there and then about who would have which stone. Instead, Raider waved his opponent on to make first choice, with a true Southern duelist's courtesy that brought a murmur of approval from the Pomos.

Then they came at one another, each holding his own stone. Raider tried to swing his at Draper's head and nearly lost his grip on it. The stone was so big and heavy, it could easily slip from his hand unless clutched tightly. It was too big for him to hold in his hand and punch with. Likewise, Draper was having some difficulties with his weapon. The two men circled each other, trying to get a feel for what they could do with these stones, while the Indians watched impassively.

Raider guessed now why the Pomos had examined the stones so carefully. They were both exactly of a size and weight to be so clumsy as to be almost useless as weapons. The most the two men could expect to do was stand nose to nose and batter each other to death. That way there would be no survivor, no victor for the Indians to keep their word to. The Pomos had it even better figured out than Raider first estimated. There was

only one thing they hadn't included in their calculations
—him.

Draper took a clumsy swipe at Raider's face with his
stone, and Raider moved his face just far enough out of
its way and no farther. But he did take a step backward.
This led Draper to take a step forward. In this way,
Raider led him where he wanted him, making occasional swings at him to keep him preoccupied with the
fight. Once near the fire, Raider made some quick steps
back, putting a few paces between them, then flung his
stone with all his force at One-Ear.

If it had been thrown at his head, Draper might have
been able to duck it. It was not. The stone caught him in
the center of the chest, pushing the wind out of his
lungs. But Draper felt his body absorb the blow. He
stayed on his feet and breathed new air in. The pain was
overcome by the knowledge that he now had a stone and
Raider had lost his.

But in the couple of seconds Draper had taken to
recover, Raider had pulled a flaming birch branch, thick
as a man's arm, from the fire. The branch, about six feet
long, was burning in the middle and broke at this point,
so that Raider was left with a blunt-pointed spear less
than three feet long, tipped by glowing embers. He advanced with this on Draper, holding the glowing end out
toward his opponent's face.

"Tell them who I am, Draper," Raider warned him.
"Tell them you're a wanted man, that you're my prisoner. Come on. I'm giving you a chance."

One-Ear tried. The English-speaking Pomo wouldn't
listen. Raider tried. While Raider was talking to the
Pomo, saying he wanted to take his prisoner to Round

Valley, One-Ear swung with his stone at the Pinkerton's head.

Raider reacted so quickly it was clear to the Indians that this had been a daring taunt on his part that Draper had been too stupid to understand. To save himself from the blow, Raider thrust upward with the tip of the smoldering branch, catching Draper with it on the throat just beneath his chin. With a savage two-handed jerk upward, the Pinkerton caused the point to rip through the soft skin, tear through the roots of his tongue, and penetrate the palate.

Raider eased the stone from Draper's limp hand and put him out of his agony by cracking open his forehead.

CHAPTER EIGHT

Sunday was the day of rest. Sometimes a preacher showed up in town and everyone turned out to hear him —very often not so much from religious feelings but only because any kind of entertainment was scarce in Rockport. This Sunday there was no visiting preacher. The men would smoke their pipes, sharpen their saws and axes, recover from Saturday night. The Eagle Timber Company's bookkeeper, Ted Malloy, didn't smoke, didn't have to sharpen anything but his pen nib, didn't have to recover because he didn't drink. His rooming house was noisy on a Sunday morning, so he liked to take himself down to the sawmill's counting-house, where he could have peace and quiet to study chess problems and read in an improving book. He resisted the temptation to work, because it was the Sabbath day; however, he felt this temptation strong in him, and it humbled him to think that he had such a powerful urge to sin. But he was strong-minded and pure, and he resisted the allure of those ledger books.

The sawmill was a very different place on a Sunday. No saws whined, no logs rolled, no men cursed or laughed. A single watchman had the place to himself. Lately, because of the troubles, Cal Blair or one or both of the Pinkertons might wander around for a spell to make sure all was in order. The watchman nodded to Malloy as he entered the compound. No one else was about. Malloy spent almost an hour analyzing a chess game he had lost to Samuel Trotter the previous day, searching for moves that might have reversed the verdict. He didn't come up with any strong ideas, so to clear his head he walked out along the sea edge. A foot of exposed dripping sea wood told him that the tide had just begun to ebb. He was surprised to see two men working at the holding pond.

The big redwoods were felled in spring and summer and sawn into logs. The logs were hauled by oxen over skid roads to the nearest river. The next flood carried the logs downriver to the sawmill. The holding pond was an enclosure around the river mouth, constructed of floating logs chained together in a semicircle, which prevented the logs newly washed down by the river from floating out to sea.

The Eagle Timber Company's holding pond was filled by logs packed into tight floating formations. On workdays, men with a skilled sense of balance walked over these logs and guided them here and there. Malloy realized that the two men he was watching now were not so sure of their footing. His eyesight was not very good, and he thought for a while the men might be

Raider and Cal Blair. When he hailed them from a distance in a friendly way, one fired a pistol shot at him.

In an instant, Malloy knew what the two men were up to—breaking the holding pond wall to release the logs on the ebb tide. He rushed back to the counting-house, hearing another gunshot behind him as he ran. He peeped out from inside and saw that the two had returned to their task, no doubt pleased they had scared him off.

But Malloy had not run because he was scared. No, sir! He had not been wasting his time. Feeling guilty about how his inept gun handling had contributed to the death of Abe Blair, Malloy had pestered Samuel Trotter to teach him the rudiments of firing a gun. Malloy was not running for fear of his life, as the two men thought. No, sir! He was running for his gun.

Behind the books on his office bookshelf now, instead of a pocket gun, lay a loaded lever-action Winchester rifle. Malloy opened a drawer and stuffed three fistfuls of loose cartridges in his pocket, then levered a shell into the chamber and headed for the door. He saw the men hammering at a chain holding the log boom and he opened fire on them.

In truth, Samuel Trotter's shooting lessons hadn't extended to the point of enabling Malloy to hit anything yet. The young Pinkerton had mainly concentrated on training Malloy not to shoot himself or others standing next to him. Things usually went well until Malloy got excited and began waving the gun barrel around or accidentally brushed his sleeve against the trigger. Someone less dedicated than Trotter would have called it quits.

The two men breaking open the holding pond didn't know this. They just saw a rifleman firing on them from the sawmill and found themselves out on the logs with nowhere to go for cover except into the water. Rather than that, they ran across the logs as fast as they could while still maintaining their balance, made it safely to dry land as the fusillade of rifle shots came their way, and escaped from the compound while the shooter was reloading.

Samuel Trotter and some other men showed up shortly after, not in time to apprehend the two men but in plenty of time for Malloy to mistake them for evil-doers. He emptied a magazine of seventeen shots at them before they managed to persuade him they were friends rather than foe.

The watchman had a bad bruise on the side of his head and was tied to a pillar inside the sawmill.

"From now on we need two men on watch outside working hours," Trotter said. "Nice shooting, Malloy. Raider will be pleased to hear about it when he gets back. You ready for another shooting lesson?"

Malloy felt tempted, but he fought it off and said firmly, "Never on Sunday."

Raider guessed he would miss the logging camp on the walk back through the woods, and he was right. It had been a full day's hard walk east to the valley where the Pomos had camped. Now he had walked a full day back west and the sun was moving toward setting. He would have to make camp soon and find something to eat. The Pomos had given him a feed of deer meat be-fore he left them that morning, and since then, what with all the walking and scrambling and having given away all his stores the previous night, he was mighty hungry.

Very little animal life was to be seen where the trees were tall—the forest was bare and dark underneath. Along streambeds and on the sides of hills, where the trees were smaller, he saw some birds, but they were too small and fast to hit with a .44 revolver. Whenever he saw squirrels, he blasted away at them. He was lucky to find one dumb enough to stand on a tree trunk staring at him. That became his evening meal, roasted over an open fire. He banked up the fire with wood, made a bed beside it of pine boughs, and fell into a deep, exhausted sleep after his two solid days of tramping. His sleep the night before had been less than sound, since he was not sure when the Pomos might suddenly decide to send him after One-Ear Draper to the Happy Hunting Ground in the Sky. But they were true to their word and gave him his gun back and parted in peace.

Raider hadn't decided yet how he would trim down the account of what happened in his report to Chicago. Allan Pinkerton almost certainly would disapprove of any operative using a smoldering stake and a stone. Maybe he'd leave out the Pomos, too—they just complicated things. A lone gunfight in the redwoods. That would be fine. Then they could close their folder on One-Ear, which would bring joy to their bureaucratic hearts. The staff at headquarters were always pleased at neat endings. Raider always tried to see that this was all they ever got from him, regardless of real facts.

Next morning he woke a bit stiff and so hungry he'd have attacked just about anything chewable and digestible. He tried to shoot another squirrel but met no animals fool enough to sit still. After some wild shots at birds, he settled for some berries and tramped on west, keeping the morning sun at his back. He knew he couldn't have very far to go. He might miss the logging camp, but he could hardly miss the Pacific Ocean.

After a couple of hours, he came to the sea all right —yet it was not what he expected. Waves beat on jagged rocks at the foot of cliffs that stretched up and down the uninhabited coast as far as he could see. He had more or less assumed he would see a sawmill when he reached the sea, but there was nothing here except seagulls, seaweed, rocks, and spray. He had no idea whether he was north or south of Rockport. A thick fog bank rolled in slowly from the sea. While he stood and watched, within fifteen minutes the entire landscape disappeared into fine gray mist. He could only hear the waves beating somewhere below him now, invisible in the fog.

He decided to walk south, knowing of only one shipping point north of Rockport, called Bear Harbor, whereas there were many to the south. The fog made the going difficult. It was never so thick that he couldn't see twenty yards or so ahead, but he had no idea where he was going unless he stayed close to the water and so had to thread his way along the edge of every headland, taking no shortcuts, if indeed there were any.

It was early afternoon when he just about staggered into a miserable little collection of shacks around a small sawmill on the mouth of a stream. After learning that its name was Usal and that he was south of Rockport, Raider was so anxious to leave the place that he didn't ask for food and hired a man with a ketch to take him to Westport, farther south again. Westport had two big sawmills and a lot of traffic. It wasn't as lively a town as Mendocino City; all the same, it was a great improvement over Rockport and Usal, and it way to hell beat walking along the rocky coast in fog.

He was so ravenous he ate a whole salmon and a loaf of sourdough bread. Then he put away a third of a bottle of peculiar-tasting whiskey. He was beginning to feel his old self once more and decided that a pretty woman would help complete his recovery.

A logger directed him to a small cabin on the side of a hill. The door was painted bright pink, and there were red flowers in little windowboxes. Raider knocked on the door and peered in through a windowpane. A woman looked back at him from inside. Raider smiled, raised his hat to her, and inclined his head toward the door. Her answer to his dumb show was one of her own. She began to disrobe before him. Raider headed for the door.

By the time he had closed it behind him, she had stripped naked and was walking toward a bed in the one-room cabin, showing him her twitching, shapely ass as she went. She lay on her back on the bed and stroked herself as she gyrated her sensuous body beneath his avid gaze. She enticed him to her with the slow and teasing thrusts of her hips.

Raider lost no time in shucking his gunbelt, boots, and clothes. He placed himself between her spread-apart thighs and shoved the swollen head of his big cock into her warm dampness.

He drove his rod into her with rhythmic abandon, and his belly slapped against hers as he forced the full length of his manhood deep inside her.

She uttered stifled gasps and sobs, thrusting back with ferocity beneath him.

The power and frequency of Raider's thrusts increased, and he grunted like a hog as his excitement and pleasure grew. Finally he exploded in a stream of hot jism inside her, feeling her begin to convulse in her own ecstasy under the force of his passion.

This time Jeff Dench did not scowl when he saw Stanton coming. Neither did he look pleased.

"Mr. Dench," Stanton began, "this thing is way out of my control. I can't handle these Pinkertons myself, and the men you sent me either got killed or they ran off because they have some sense. I've lost my warehouse. When I tried to start up my business again, I found the lumbermen won't deal with me because Cal Blair has put the word out I'm trying to wreck the Eagle Timber Company. We ain't winning this war, Mr. Dench, no matter what way you look at it."

"What about that fella we set up so he could kill Raider?"

"He's dead," Stanton said, not wasting time on explanations his boss would not want to hear.

"How about the holding pond?"

"Two men I put on that job were lucky to escape with their lives. They're both working in a logging camp now and say they don't want to hear no more from me."

"Why?" Dench asked.

Stanton looked exasperated. He almost shouted, "Because every damn man I put on the job gets shot, beaten, or chased off. The Eagle Timber Company's built itself a mean reputation with those two Pinkertons hanging around. They been an influence on everyone there. You got all kinds of workers there now toting guns and spoiling for a fight. If things keep going this way, Mr. Dench, you're going to need the cavalry to move in on 'em and root 'em out."

"I'm disappointed, Stanton."

"Well, I'm way more than disappointed, Mr. Dench. I'm dang near destroyed."

"I thought you could handle this for me."

"What you need out here, sir, is General Lee or General Sherman. I done all I could with what you provided me."

Dench registered the fact that Stanton was not play-acting. He seemed genuinely annoyed at having been asked to do the impossible and then being blamed for not having achieved it. This was Dench's favorite method of handling those who worked for him, and he had developed, over the years, a keen sense of how far he could push a man. Stanton was still willing. However, he needed now to be faced in a new direction before being pushed from behind once more.

"Maybe we need to look at what we're doing, Stanton," Dench said magnanimously. "Maybe you're right when you say you've done all you can with what I've given you. I don't know why two lone Pinkertons should be too much for you and your men to handle, but this is what you say, and I have to believe you. All right, if we accept the fact that we can't take out these Pinkertons or Cal Blair, who's protected by them, what can we do?"

"Right now, I dunno."

"That's not what I want to hear, Stanton," Jeff Dench said sharply. "Bring down the logging operation. Wreck that mill. All I need is the redwoods, Stanton. I can rebuild everything else. Smash everything if you can't bury those men. I'm paying you top dollar."

"Yes, sir."

From Manchester, Stanton brought back five hired guns to Mendocino City in his sailboat. He sailed close to shore as they passed Little River to show the men the sawmill and compound. Stanton anchored the boat at its usual place off Mendocino City, brought the men ashore in the dinghy, and led them to a saloon on Main Street where they could have drinks while he found them lodgings.

He was kind of unlucky to run into Raider on the boardwalk just before they reached the saloon. Raider had been celebrating his return from up Rockport way with Silas Hanks in about a dozen saloons. They were walking shoulder to shoulder along the boardwalk, smiles on their faces, feeling on top of the world. One or the other of them would give way when they met someone coming against them on the boardwalk. They were all politeness and good nature. Until they saw Stanton and his five new guns coming toward them.

Stanton hesitated a moment, then kept coming, saying over his shoulder to the men behind him in a low voice, "Trouble ahead, boys."

None of the five men had to ask where. They could see it coming at them in the form of a big, rough-looking hombre with a black hat and a low-slung Remington .44. They could see too the big state-of-Maine woodsman next to him, who also wore a gun and who had hands big enough to dig a man's grave with. A dozen paces behind these two, they spotted a third man carry-

ing a repeating rifle; he was small and wore specs over
his eyes and walked real steady and sober—the sort
who killed with a smile and a pardon-me. Like Stanton
said, trouble ahead.

Raider swept Stanton out of his way with a brush of
his arm, like he was of no more account than a towel
hanging on a clothesline. The lightly built Stanton was
knocked from the boardwalk to the dusty street, a couple of feet below, where he landed on his backside.

The man behind Stanton stepped down off the boardwalk fast to avoid a confrontation. But the gun behind
him, a burly man with a thick neck and bushy mustaches, held his ground. Raider pushed Silas a little to
one side with his left hand, indicating that he would
handle this, and on a fair one-to-one basis. Without
breaking stride, the Pinkerton whacked his fist into the
man's gut, and the man fell off the boardwalk as he
staggered back.

He wasn't hit that hard, though, and, recovering
quickly, he made a move for his gun. Raider's left hand
dived to his Remington handle. The man was impressed
by the speed and made a show of removing his hand
from the vicinity of his own revolver. When the remaining three men on the boardwalk saw this, they stepped
down into the street without waiting to be challenged.

Raider and Silas Hanks walked on, with Samuel
Trotter and his rifle bringing up the rear.

Stanton, still sitting in the dirt, cussed out the five
so-called desperadoes Dench had given him to wipe out
the Eagle Timber Company.

CHAPTER NINE

"If I send you back, you don't get paid," Stanton told the five men in the cabin he had rented for them on the edge of Mendocino City. They had come from San Francisco to Manchester, and then from Manchester to here, without knowing who was hiring them beyond Stanton. "What I say goes," Stanton continued. "I promised you good money for results. I didn't promise you nothing for being too yaller to fight a man who throws me off the boardwalk. It was six of us against two of them—"

"Five of us," one man corrected him, "since you wasn't in a position to do much fighting, sitting on your ass in the dirt. And there was three of them, counting the one following behind."

"That's still five against three," Stanton snapped back. "What's wrong? You can't even handle them with the odds in your favor?"

131

"Not them three, we can't. You said we wasn't going to be up against no professional gunfighters. Just destroying property was all. That's what you said."

"Maybe I did," Stanton conceded, "but we can't let them push us around like that. They been trying to run me out of town. The big Pinkerton who shoved me was the one who dynamited my warehouse. I tried to prove it to the marshal, but I didn't have any witnesses to stand by me. Raider is his name. He told the marshal he had no hard evidence against me and promised to take no action against me until he had—making it sound like it would only be a matter of time. I think he'd have shot me by now except my complaints to the marshal put him in a position where he had to be careful. He was just looking for an excuse to start a fight on the boardwalk."

"So he could kill us all," one man said gloomily. "I don't mind breaking up stuff, but I ain't here to outgun no shootists."

"None of us is, Stanton," another added.

"All right, all right, but you don't have to act so yellow," Stanton told them. "He knows now you're all scared of him, and he'll come round to kick ass any time he feels like it. If he shows up at this cabin, I'm depending on you boys to fill him full of lead or take the next schooner out."

"Instead of just yapping at us, Stanton, why don't you tell us what you want done, so we can do it and you can quit complaining?"

"Fair enough," Stanton said. "I'll put you lot on the job first thing tomorrow, and then we'll see what you five are made of."

* * *

Jeff Dench drove a horse and buggy to the Manchester landing cove to meet the passengers off the ship from San Francisco. Two men in dark clothes shook his hand, put their valises up behind, and climbed onto the buggy.

"How's business?" Dench asked.

"Going great. It couldn't be better."

"No problems?" Dench inquired.

"Nothing that we two can't handle for you."

Dench nodded, pleased. "What are they saying about me down in the city these days?"

The two men in dark clothes exchanged a glance before one said, "The lawyers are handling that, and they tell me things are not going as smoothly as they had hoped. But you know what lawyers are like. They won't be rushed."

"What's not going smoothly?" Dench wanted to know.

"Jeff, we're the managers of your construction business. What do we know about law? Why don't you have us send up one of those slippery-tongued shysters to explain to you himself. We brought the ledgers with us on the buildings your company has been constructing. We couldn't be doing better. And those legal problems are not affecting us in any way. So what do we know about anything?"

"I know they're fixing to make charges against me," Dench said. "They won't make them while I'm gone, in case I don't come back. But all I have to do is show my face, then they'll arrest me and try to hold me without bond. There's men in that town who want me hung. They're the ones behind all this."

"Sure they are," one of his managers agreed. "It's all a political thing."

"That's what I'm thinking," Dench said. "That girl was only a whore anyhow. She didn't have nobody. So why all the fuss? It was only an accident she died."

"Could've happened to anyone," one of the managers agreed.

"So the lawyers are against me coming back right now?" Dench asked.

The two managers exchanged another look. One said, "Some of them were suggesting Manchester might not be far enough away. They thought you should cross the state line—"

"I can't do that," Dench protested. "I have to look after my business. Up here at least I can take care of the timber supply while you two do the building." He paused for a moment. "But it mightn't be a bad idea to move a bit farther north up the coast, away from the city. I've been thinking of acquiring a mill up there, near where I have timber rights. I reckon if I was to spend a year up there, them lawyers could get around to fixing things for me in San Francisco."

Cal Blair put some papers in front of Raider. He said, "It's an offer for my company. Look at who it's from." His index finger rested beneath a name.

"No surprise," Raider said. "It had to be Dench all along. Now that Stanton's not doing so well, he's seeing if he can buy you out fair and square. Is the offer good?"

"Not when you count my brother's death into it."

"I wasn't suggesting you were considering it," Raider said. "What I need to know is whether the money is generous and this is a peace offer or whether the bid is low and backed by more trouble."

"Not generous, not low. I believe he'd go much higher if he thought I'd sell outright to him. I'm going to turn him down."

"Don't," Raider said.

"What?"

"Don't communicate with him at all. Send no messages. If he wants to bargain, let him come here."

"I might end by shooting the bastard," Cal warned.

"He'll take care you don't get the chance. I'd like to get a look at him. Stanton is a no-account little runt. Step on him and Dench will send in someone else. It's Dench we need to bring here. I could probably get more out of him up here than down in Manchester. You say nothing. We'll wait and see what he does."

"They'll never expect us to come this way," Stanton told the five men. "I have it all worked out. We do it tonight. Better bring your things with you. I reckon we won't be coming back here."

They ate and had a few drinks before leaving Mendocino City in Stanton's sailboat. The sun was setting, a huge copper ball, into the calm sea. The boat sailed straight out, due west, until darkness fell. Then they turned around, and this time Stanton headed a little to the south of Mendocino City, to bring him to Little River. They could see nothing now except the lights along the coast—a big group of them at Mendocino City and a much smaller number at Little River.

The five hired guns were no sailors, yet they knew there would be problems in darkness with the rocks on the shore, even with the sea this calm.

"Don't worry," Stanton told them. "I know this coastline like the back of my hand, and I been working out this approach for some time. You leave it to me. I'll take you in and bring you out without so much as scraping a rock. Remember, this is my boat. It ain't you five I'm concerned over—I wouldn't want to hurt her."

A bit more reassured, they watched the lights on shore grow closer and heard the slap of water on invisible spikes of sharp rock which they knew stuck out of the water at odd places all around them. Stanton kept his eyes on the shore. He was the only one not peering nervously into the dark, waiting for a jagged gray shape to suddenly loom out of the night and crack the hull like an eggshell. He worked the sails and the wheel by himself and brought the unlighted craft silently through the darkness beneath the chute used to load planks on schooners. No ships were at anchor here.

Stanton was able to bring his sailboat into much shallower water than the much deeper-drafted schooners could enter. He dropped the main and fore sails and relied on a small triangular aft sail to bring the boat slowly to a large rock. He then spun the wheel and lowered the aft sail. This maneuver caused the stern to swing around and the boat to sidle gently against the rock. One man stepped onto it and held the craft there with a length of rope.

Everything was gestures now. Stanton had stopped their talking fifteen minutes previously, explaining how sounds, even whispers, traveled clearly for great distances over calm water at night.

The four other men and Stanton climbed out of the boat onto the rock and crossed the marshy ground behind it to the sawmill. There was no sign of the two watchmen they knew were on duty—they would be keeping an eye on the landward side, not guessing any intruders would come from open water through the rock-strewn shallows. Stanton's heart began to beat uncontrollably fast, and not from fear but from the prospect of having revenge—his own personal vengeance—so close at hand. Dench was paying for this, but it was Stanton's pleasure.

Before setting sail that evening, he had sent one man to buy eighteen sticks of dynamite, blasting caps, and fuse. He had inserted caps and fuse in six sticks and bound two extra sticks to each of these six. His warehouse had been dynamited and burned to the ground. Now he was going to repay this injury in kind.

He moved quickly with the four men inside the dark sawmill, entering by way of a runway for logs. Not knowing exactly where to find what, they picked the six biggest machines they could make out, placed a charge of three sticks somewhere in each, and paid out fuse behind them as they moved on. They spent a great deal of time bumping into each other and protecting the stretched-out fuses from one another, but at last they got the job done and ended with six separate fuse ends at their entry point. Stanton connected the six loose ends to a single strand of fuse and paid this out over the marshy ground as they moved toward the boat.

Stanton waved the men ahead of him. He heard them climb the rock and heard their muffled footsteps on board the boat. No alarm had been raised. They had come and gone without being seen. Exactly what he wanted. Those Pinkertons wouldn't know what had hit them. He savored the moment with a smile, then stooped, struck a match, and lit the fuse.

The sails were raised and the boat was going out to sea when the first charge blew. They saw its orange glow as it blew out all the windows of the sawmill. This blast was followed by the others in rapid succession.

Several fires started, and flames illuminated the water near the sawmill. Stanton's sailboat had already traveled too far out to be revealed in this light. They had come and gone like destroying angels. For the first time in a long while, Stanton felt back at the helm, in control of things.

All Little River heard the explosions and rushed to the sawmill to quench the fires. After hours of confusion and hard work, they saved the mill building and other structures, plus the planks and uncut lumber. As soon as things looked as if they were being brought under control, Raider beckoned to Samuel Trotter and they took a horse and wagon in to Mendocino City. The horse knew the trail, and they hung an oil lantern on each side of the wagon to light the way. The cabin where the five men were staying was empty and bare. Likewise, Stanton had checked out of his hotel the previous afternoon. On the off chance they might show up, the two Pinkertons split up, Trotter watching the hotel, Raider the cabin. At daylight they gave up and went back to Little River on the wagon.

On the way, they stopped off at the dynamite factory. No, nothing had been sold to Stanton since they last talked. There was a stranger yesterday, though, who had bought eighteen sticks. He didn't say who he was with. Sure, he could have been working for Stanton.

The full extent of the damage at the sawmill was now evident to everyone in daylight. Six of the big saws and log splitters were damaged beyond repair, being left as tangled masses of iron. None of the other damage was severe. Raider and Trotter carefully examined the compound fences, which Trotter had recently reinforced, without finding any sign of entry.

"One or both of them watchmen has gotta be in on this," Raider said.

Samuel nodded.

"One of them was the fella who got hit on the head and tied to a pillar the time Malloy stopped them breaking open the holding pond."

"Let's find him."

When they located him, he was just about to leave for home and catch some sleep after a long night of fighting fires and cleaning up.

"We all been up all night," Raider snarled, pushing him against a wall. "Listen to me careful now. This is the second time you been sleeping on the job when Stanton's goons arrived."

"I wasn't sleeping! There was two of us. Neither of us saw nothing. First time, I was alone and they snuck up behind and knocked me cold. When I woke, I was tied up. This time I saw nothing, heard nothing, knew nothing—until that dynamite started to kick."

"How did you know it was dynamite? No one said it was dynamite."

"They don't have to," the watchman said. "I spent four years mining over in Calaveras County, and I know dynamite when I hear it."

Raider pulled him outside by the arm, treating him roughly, causing workers to stare and talk among themselves. "You're too slick a talker for me to believe," Raider said. "You seen that fence. They didn't come through that. We just been all around it, so we know. That leaves us with two possibilities. Either you and your buddy was asleep on the job or you let those hombres in through the gates."

"No way! We both was awake. We let no one in. I swear!"

"How come I just don't believe you?" Raider asked.

"'Cause you gotta find how they done it. If you can't blame us watchmen, who've you left to blame? You'd have to admit you just don't know. And you'd never want to do that."

"I don't want you getting saucy with me," Raider grated. "I don't like you. If some of those folks were to get mad enough to put a rope around your neck, it wouldn't keep me awake at night wondering if they got the wrong man."

"I been doing the best I can," the watchman said in a whiney voice. "You're just looking for a fall guy to make you look good, like you're doing your job. You don't give a damn. I'm an innocent man!"

"I don't," Raider bellowed at him, "'cause you ain't!"

"Fuck you!"

Raider stumbled against the watchman accidentally on purpose. They were walking next to the holding pond, and the watchman fell into its deep water. He disappeared beneath the surface for a few moments, then his head popped up and he yelled, clutching at the side, "I can't swim! Help! Dear God, help me! I don't wanna drown!"

Trotter rushed over and grabbed his coat collar. The watchman clutched with panicky strength to the young

Pinkerton's arm. Raider put the sole of his boot on the man's face and pressed his head slowly below water.

"Raider! Are you crazy?" Trotter shouted. "Help me pull him out."

"Sweet Jesus, help me!" the man shouted when his head popped up again.

Trotter got a firm hold on him.

Raider raised his boot to kick the watchman's head.

"No! No!" the man shouted. "I know how they done it. Water! Water!"

"You ain't coming out till you tell me," Raider snarled. "You either learn to tell the truth or you learn to swim. You don't have much time either way."

"I'm telling you," the man told him, coughing with water in his lungs. "Water!"

"Okay, pull him out," Raider said to Trotter. "If this don't make sense, he goes back in. You hear that?" he shouted to the watchman.

"Help!"

Trotter hauled the man out and sat him on the ground.

The watchman pointed toward the sea. "Water," he said. "They came in Stanton's sailboat. I didn't see them. I only thought of it when you pushed me in."

Raider saw the truth of this explanation immediately. He looked down at the soaked, shivering man and said impatiently, "It took you long enough to think of it."

Raider walked slowly back to the sawmill, considering the possibilities. He saw Cal Blair talking with the schooner captain Midnight Olsen, who said he had come straight down from Mendocino City once he heard the news. Raider said he wanted to talk to him and asked him to wait. To Cal he said quietly, "Don't argue with me. Do as I say. Tell the same to Trotter—only don't let anyone hear you. We've talked with one watchman. Is the second one here?"

Blair pointed to a tall thin man with a fringe of beard around the outline of his face.

Raider walked over and took him roughly by the arm. "I'm taking you in for some hard questioning. Your buddy's just been telling us some stories about you two last night. If I have my way, you two will be behind bars until you're both old men."

Raider dragged him along, and the unfortunate man was too shocked to manage more than a few half-stifled protests. Raider brought him against his will to meet Trotter and the man he had rescued from the holding pond. Trotter was assisting him by supporting his arm, although it now looked as though he had placed him under arrest too.

Raider said in a loud voice to Trotter, so all the workers nearby could hear, "Take this one along too. Get that man a change of clothes before you lock him up. Then stand close guard over the pair of them until I relieve you. Cal Blair will go along with you."

Trotter's mouth opened and closed like a fish's breathing water. But by now if a fountain of fiery lava had erupted from the top of Raider's hat, Trotter would have thought about it for a while before he drew definite conclusions. From Raider's point of view, this meant that Trotter had finally picked up some real genius training as a Pinkerton operative—meaning he had learned not to mess with Raider.

Cal went with him, taking the two men into custody. Out of the corner of his eye, Raider registered the response of the men standing around, which was that the Pinkertons had pinned something on the two men regarding the sawmill blasts.

Taking Midnight Olsen with him, Raider left the compound and wandered along the shoreline toward the shipbuilding yards, where men constructed schooners at the water's edge, propping them up on their keels on dry land with supporting redwood beams.

Raider gestured to a little dinghy, with its oars hanging in the oarlocks. "You row. I do better on a horse."

. Midnight Olsen was never averse to putting out to sea, whatever the reason, so long as the weather was favorable. He rowed straight out, with short economical strokes, the oar blades barely feathering the water.

"Stop here," Raider said, when they were a good distance out but could see the approach to the Eagle Lumber Company clearly. "You know Stanton's sailboat. Tell me, how would you bring that boat straight to that sawmill in pitch darkness without running up on any rocks?"

At dusk the two watchmen were still under lock and key in a company storage house. Raider saw to it that both were fed and kindly treated, bringing them a whiskey bottle from Cal's store to help them pass the time.

"But no singing or laughing," he warned them. "I want word to get back to Stanton that we're holding you two for being in cahoots with him. If he thinks we haven't figured out how he did it, I'm betting on him coming back tonight before we do get around to it."

The two men were quite agreeable once they learned they were not really under suspicion, although they breathed easier after Raider had left.

He had rounded up eight teams of two men, including Samuel, Cal, and Silas. The other thirteen were trusted lumber company employees. None of them as yet knew what Raider was up to or what he had in mind for them. Each man carried two horse blankets and two lanterns.

Just before dusk, following a map that Raider and Midnight Olsen had drawn, they went around the town nailing up horse blankets over certain windows and placing hurricane lamps in certain places. A man stayed at each location, either to make sure the blankets weren't removed or that the lamps stayed lit and in place.

"Shoot any bastard who interferes," Raider ordered in a voice loud enough for skulking would-be interferers to hear.

When everything was in place, he went down alone to the sawmill compound. It was dark. He was immediately challenged by the four watchmen on duty for that night. He complimented them on their alertness and told them to keep a close watch on the gate. He'd keep an eye out round back.

It was totally dark by the time he got down to where the calm water was lapping against the rocks and the seaweed smell assailed his nostrils. He looked back at the lights of the town, which all shone bright, safe, and normal.

After their successful raid of the night before, Stanton sailed south and anchored in a lonely cove with a sheltered beach. They slept the night there and lazed away a good part of the day. Plenty of fresh water and a week's supply of food had been stowed in the sailboat's cabin, along with whiskey, beer, and tobacco.

One man said, "If we'd brought some women, life would be complete."

Everyone's attitude had changed from frustration and suspicion to comradely good humor. Stanton preened to find himself acknowledged and respected as leader. It made him feel generous and expansive, and what he had seen before as cowardice and shortcomings in his men he now saw as personal quirks or human failings.

The two men he sent to buy chickens and eggs from a small logging camp farther up the coast came back with the news that Stanton had been blamed for the raid and that the two watchmen had been arrested by the Pinkertons for involvement in the crime. This news put Stanton to thinking. As leader, it was his burden to come up with fresh, successful ideas. That's what leaders were for. They were one jump ahead of the rest of mankind, maybe even two or three jumps sometimes. Stanton would settle for one jump.

What the man said set him to thinking. If the Pinkertons were blaming the watchmen, they believed Stanton had come in the gates. Sooner or later, they would find out differently. A clever leader would take advantage of this somehow. Not to go into the sawmill again—that would be guarded. No, the thing to exploit was the seaward approach.

"We're going back tonight," he said to the men, pleased at the incredulous looks this brought to their faces. He explained his reasoning and described their target. "We can catch most of the ebb flow even if we come in two hours after dark. This time we don't touch on land at all. We just sail in to the edge of the holding pond, silently unlatch some of the chains holding the boom in place, and the tide will do our work for us. Those logs will be scattered high and wide, and the ones they do get back will be nearly worthless because of damage by rocks."

The men thought this was a good idea and readily went along with his plans. They set off in the boat at sunset and arrived at Little River as they planned, about two hours after dark. Sailing without running lights, the sailboat approached the shore at a good clip with an onshore breeze.

Stanton took his bearings on the lights on the shore. He now had full confidence in his navigational abilities and followed the course in that he had taken the previous night. With watch in hand, he sailed for a certain number of minutes with certain lights aligned, then bore down on a different light for another fixed amount of time, changing to yet another bearing on the alignment of another pair of lights.

The boat was going at more than eight knots under main and fore sails when she struck a rock. The jagged edge stove in the side. The boat immediately began to take on water and listed heavily to port. Two men had been flung overboard by the impact. Those still on deck were almost waist deep in water.

Stanton ignored all this. He stood on the deck of his sinking vessel and stared fixedly at the shore. He shouted, "Those rotten, cheating sons of bitches changed the lights on me. Wreckers! Murderers!"

CHAPTER TEN

The two men knocked into the water by the impact of Stanton's sailboat on the rocks were presumed drowned. Stanton and the three others climbed onto the prow, wedged firmly on the rocks, as the rest of the boat sank beneath the surface. They stayed there till the tide was fully out, when they were able to wade ashore through chest-deep water.

They came on shore at the boat-building slips and headed for the nearest saloon for a hot spiced punch to get the blood flowing in their veins. The appearance of four drenched, cold men, bleeding from rock cuts, would normally have caused everyone to come to their aid. The fact that this was Stanton and his men caused only a stony silence. Stanton wasn't welcome in Little River. If he and his men had walked into the town in good health and in dry clothes, they would have found trouble quick. Looking half dead like they did, no one picked on them—yet.

"Keep them here," one man said in a whisper to the bartender. "I seen one of the Pinkertons with a lamp up the town a little while back. Maybe he was looking for them."

The man slipped away and brought Samuel Trotter and some others to the saloon. Trotter disarmed them and held them there while someone went to find Raider. Raider was still sitting on a rock by the water's edge, his carbine across his knees, looking out into the darkness, when the man found him.

He smiled when he heard the news. "I never heard anything here. It must have happened to them a ways out, I reckon. There was some shouts a long while back, but I couldn't be sure what direction they were coming from."

First thing he did was to order the man to tell the others to remove the blankets from the windows and douse the lamps. He didn't want any innocent mariners going aground. When he got to the saloon, a sheriff's deputy was there. He had listened to Stanton's theory about his "accident" and asked Raider if he had any charges to make against Stanton and his men.

"No charges," Raider answered, though those words stuck in his throat. The reality was, however, that there was not a thing he could prove against Stanton or these men. He didn't even have enough against them to hold them for a night in jail.

When the sheriff's deputy heard this, and knowing how feelings ran about Stanton in Little River, he offered to escort them by wagon to Mendocino City, leaving right away.

Stanton didn't hang around to have one for the road.

"That slimebag just walked out of here," Raider complained to Cal Blair next morning over four eggs, inch-thick slices of smoky, salty bacon, a salmon cutlet, and a half dozen biscuits, washed down by coffee that had a kick to it like white lightning.

Cal was celebrating the previous night's happenings, not complaining. "Damn, Raider, they can't call you 'cowboy' no more. That sure was a stroke of genius, moving them lights. I think you got the sea in your blood. You ever thought of buying yourself a schooner and shipping timber?"

"The more I see of that goddamn water," Raider said, "the more I dream of grass. It's flat and green too, like the sea, but you can put pieces of it between your teeth and chew it."

"I think maybe it's too late for you to get the call of the sea. A lot of times myself I'd like to sell this sawmill and buy me a boat, like Midnight Olsen's or Portwine Ellefsen's. You know them boys. That's the life, Raider. Only my wife and kids don't think so."

"All in all, maybe you have the best deal," Raider said.

"It's easy for a bachelor like you to tell that to a married man," Cal said jokingly. "Of course, if you really believe it, I hear there's a widow woman who's taken a fancy to you. If you was to hitch up with her, you'd find you owned half a sawmill and some fine timber rights."

Raider was taken aback. He had been very discreet. He said, "Do you mind if I inquire who or what put these thoughts in your head?"

"My wife." Cal laughed. "It takes one woman to figure out another. So far as I know, nothing's been said between them—they're not close friends. I suppose it's mostly guesswork on my wife's part, but usually she's one helluva shrewd guesser. She keeps me on my best behavior, 'cause I know sure as hell she'd find me out. Most of the time, anyhow."

"Well, if I was to get the urge to settle down," Raider said in a friendly way, "I couldn't do no better anywhere than here. If we could flatten all them mountains out, get rid of the trees and rocks, and bring in some cattle and horses on sweet grass, I'd be sorely tempted. No, Cal, my heart is six, seven hundred miles from here, the other side of the Rockies."

"Cowboy!"

They both laughed at that.

Raider carried on, "It really dragged me down, having to let Stanton go like that. The bastard has been a crook all his time here, and I don't have a single charge to make that will stick. How about something he's done in the past? Tell me about that swindle he worked on where Jeff Dench picked up the timber rights in these parts."

"Well, if Stanton wasn't such a gambler, going down to San Francisco and blowing his wad, even losing big sums at the tables in Mendocino City, Jeff Dench would never have laid his hands on those timber rights. Stanton had them all to himself—then I guess he got in some trouble on one of his trips to San Francisco and Dench happened to be there to bail him out."

"How did Stanton come by these timber rights in the first place?" the Pinkerton wanted to know.

"The Homestead Act was improved in '78 by the Timber and Stone Act. Stanton would go into the forest and take out location papers on suitable stands of trees. Then when a couple of schooners came to town, he'd bring every man jack of them to the county courthouse to take out their first papers, declaring their intention of becoming U.S. citizens if they wasn't so already. After that he'd bring them to the land office—maybe twenty-five men at a time—and file their claims with the location papers. Next he'd bring them to a notary public, have each of them execute an acknowledgment of a blank deed for the sum of fifty dollars. The seamen blew the money, forgot the incident, and sailed out on their ships. Stanton could later fill in the description of the claim and the transfer of title to anyone he wanted to sell it to—for whatever price he had in mind."

"He got away with it?"

"Sure he did. And a lot of others, too." Cal grinned. "You don't want to ask none of us how we put together our timber rights on public land."

"So if Stanton hadn't been a gambler, he'd have had his own sawmill and been one of the big men hereabouts?"

"Maybe the biggest," Cal confirmed. "He's got a better business head on his shoulders than any of the rest of us. Me, I'm just a logger who was always careful and had some lucky breaks. My brother, the same thing. But not Stanton. He never in his life raised blisters on his palms hefting an ax handle."

"So there's no way you see to bring charges against him on his land deals?" Raider asked.

"None at all. Maybe you should go after Dench instead."

Raider shook his head. "Stanton has to go before I can draw out Dench."

Samuel Trotter came back to Little River in the late afternoon with the information that Stanton and his three surviving men (the bodies of the other two had washed up on the rocks with the afternoon tide) had spent the previous night in their cabin in Mendocino City. They had dried their clothes in the morning sun, visited a barber and two saloons, and then ate lunch. After their meal, they bought guns, ammunition, food, and whiskey. They were last seen heading into the woods on four rented horses.

"I sent a rider to warn the men at the logging camp and on the skid roads," Samuel said.

"You did right," Raider told him. "What we have to figure now is whether they're going to make trouble in the woods or try to fool us by circling back on the sawmill. Me and Silas Hanks will go into the woods after them tomorrow morning. You and Cal Blair defend the sawmill."

Trotter wanted to go into the woods along with Raider, but he knew better than to argue.

The two men had dinner in a Little River eating house. As always in this place, it was salmon, potatoes, and beans.

"That's one thing I'll say for the prairies," Raider said reverently, "there's no goddamn salmon."

"I like it," Trotter said.

"You would."

After the meal, Trotter stayed on to play chess with

Ted Malloy. Raider looked into the Skid Row and talked for a while with some loggers and seamen. He was wondering if he shouldn't maybe pay a visit to Brenda. Maybe Cal saw wedding bells for them, but that was only because Cal hadn't seen her sling him out the last time he was there and tell him not to come back. She might do the same tonight. However, tomorrow he was going into the woods, and there was no telling how long he'd be in there, with no woman to comfort him. It was worth a try.

She had got mad at him before when she found some scratches on his shoulder and back. Raider was being genuine when he claimed he had probably gotten them from tree branches on his long walk through the woods before or after catching up with One-Ear Draper. She said a tree that could scratch like a woman had not yet been created. Raider told her there were some mighty strange trees deep in the woods. That was when she threw his shirt out the open window, followed by his left boot, and began screaming at him to go and never come back.

Brenda opened the door to his knock, smiled as if all were forgotten, and let him in. They talked in her parlor for a while, Raider perched uneasily on the delicate furniture. Careful as he was being, he still managed to smash a little china dog when he threw his hat down. He mentioned he would be going into the woods next day and might be there for a spell.

"More scratches?" she asked. "Be careful of those tree branches."

Regardless of the consequences, Raider needed to get one thing clear between them. "You know, Brenda, I ain't the settling-down kind."

"I figured as much."

"I don't know where Mr. Pinkerton is going to send me next. It could be Amarillo, Texas, or St. Joseph, Missouri. When I get that call, I gotta leave pronto."

"I'm going to miss you, Raider. Don't let's talk about it now."

"I don't want to neither, I just want it clear between you and me."

"I've always known you would have to go," she said softly, putting her hand on his arm.

In a little while they went up the staircase to her bedroom. She lay on the bed, and he kissed her and his hands caressed her body beneath her dress. She was well protected by petticoats and stays. Raider untied the bow on her dress beneath her breasts, and both of them fell out with their erect brown nipples.

Brenda was proud of her breasts, and she had a right to be. The orbs of flesh looked soft and yielding, yet they were firm to touch. His tongue sent tremors through her body, first through one nipple, then the other. He alternated between them like a man unable to make up his mind which of the pair he liked best.

She pushed him away from her and slowly began to peel off her garments. As her shapely young body emerged, he ran his hands tenderly over it, enjoying the feel of her soft skin. As he did this, she began to take off his clothes. Her fingers worked quickly and excitedly. Raider felt her long nails glide over his skin, then he almost yelped when her nails savagely raked his chest.

"Bitch!" he hissed and saw blood trickling down onto his belly.

She licked the red trickles off his chest and tongued

the scratches. Meanwhile her fingers wandered caressingly over his body, making his scalp tingle and his prick stiffen to its full length. She murmured in appreciation and took his cock in her left hand, enclosing its shaft tightly, touching the moist sensitive parts of its head with the moistened fingertips of her right hand.

Stretched beside her, he ran his tongue over her cool, perfumed skin. He licked and savored the taste of her. He kissed her full lips and thrust his tongue into her mouth. His hand crept up along the soft inside of her thigh and stroked the warm thatch of hair over her moist opening.

He worked his fingers inside her pussy until she grew frantic with lust. She clutched his hips and urgently pulled his belly toward hers. When he let the weight of his body press down on her, she trembled beneath him, parted her thighs, and raised her knees to present herself to him.

He slowly pushed the head and shaft of his manhood into her pleading inner depths. She moaned and twisted in ecstasy. The harder and faster he drove into her, the more she shuddered and groaned.

Then her entire body was seized in trembling so violent that Raider had to ease his powerful thrusting and let her climax subside, his rock-hard cock still embedded deep in her core.

Next morning she fed him a hearty breakfast, and he left before first light. He kicked on the door of Silas Hanks's twelve-by-sixteen redwood shack until he rousted him. Raider had a second breakfast and a quart of beer with him at the eating house. They saddled up and rode into the forest before daylight had fully spread across the sky. When they reached the logging camp, the cook still had some fried salmon left from breakfast. Silas ate his hungrily, but Raider hardly more than picked at his.

Raider and Silas went to see the bull bucker, as the chopping boss was called. He was the one who planned the strips of trees to be cut. The men who felled the trees were known as choppers, and they worked in pairs. It might take a pair of choppers anywhere from one to three months to clear a strip.

"When I got word yesterday that Stanton might be coming in, I passed out a rifle to each man," the bull bucker told them. "At every work site, at least one man is doing guard duty. They like that—nothing to do but sit on their ass all day and stare into the trees."

"One or two of them might have an unpleasant surprise coming their way," Raider said.

"Most of them know Stanton well enough to recognize him," the bull bucker said dismissively. "If he shows his face here, we'll take it off the front of his head."

Raider grinned. "You'd be doing me a real favor."

"If you and Silas are going to be staying here with us, you better take a look about and let the boys know you're here. You know where the boys are working, Silas."

"Sure," Silas replied and walked away with Raider. "We should take a look at the skid roads first, since that's where they attacked before."

The river was the only source of transportation for the logs down to the sawmill on the coast. For most of the year its water was too low to wash down the big logs. The snowmelt of late spring and early summer could always be depended on to provide a flood—sometimes one so great it broke the boom of the mill's holding pond. At other times of year, big rainstorms caused the flood waters. The logs were taken from the strips along skid roads, hauled by teams of oxen, and left on the riverbed, ready whenever nature was. Most of the skid roads were merely branches off the main long one, the one Stanton's men had dynamited previously. The bullpunchers carried rifles, but there wasn't much more in the line of protection that could be done for them.

"Stanton will want to scare them away to work someplace else at the same pay without the risk," Raider said.

"I don't know about that," Silas said. "That's what he tried before, and it didn't work. These bullpunchers are ornery critters. The more Stanton tries to force them to leave, the more determined they'll be to stay. Stanton knows this now. I reckon he'll be after the choppers this time. They don't have loyalty except to the tree they happen to be working on. When that's down, it's all the same if the next tree is ten miles up the coast. If I was Stanton, I'd try to chase them out."

Raider had developed a great respect for Silas's opinions. On the open range, Raider wanted no one else's opinion. He didn't know the woods like these men did, and he was willing to listen to advice. He said, "Show me."

While they were walking through the trees, a dynamite blast shook the ground under their feet. Raider's gun was in his hand.

"More'n likely, they're just splitting a log that's too big to fit on the skid road," Silas said casually. "You hear a lot of that out here. Bastards set it off without much warning, too."

Raider was kind of doubtful about not stopping to check, but he took Silas's word for it and followed him.

They came to a place where a newly felled redwood had left "a hole in the sky," as the choppers called it—a big gap in the green canopy far overhead. The Pinkerton was surprised by the amount of equipment these two men used, which they told him was all their own property: two double-bit axes, one twelve-foot and two eight-foot saws, two dozen plates, a dozen shims, ten wedges, two sledgehammers, a pair of gun sticks, a plumb bob, twelve springboards, and six pieces of staging.

When they moved on they saw some of this equipment in use. Two men were felling a redwood about fifteen feet in diameter. Since the base of the tree swelled even thicker, the cut was about ten feet above the ground. Beneath the cut, springboards were inserted in notches hacked into the trunk. Then men stood on staging planks laid across pairs of springboards. They said they had been working three days on this one tree. The forecut came first, then the deep cut. At this stage they were using a twelve-foot cross saw—shorter than the tree's diameter—and two double-bit axes, with which most of the work was done.

The tree being felled was on a slope. The choppers paused in their work when they heard a sharp crack. They said they had about fifteen minutes of chopping left and explained how they were felling the tree uphill so the trunk would have less distance to travel and thus hit the ground less heavily. Redwood timber was soft and was damaged easily. They had laid down what they called a bedding for the tree—many small trees felled and laid in its path to break its fall with their branches and leaves. This had required leveling a large area around the big redwood.

"How can you be so sure it's gonna fall that way?" Raider asked.

The two choppers took this as an insult. One cut a stake with his axe and tapped it into the ground about a hundred feet from the base of the tree.

"That tree is gonna hit that stake on the head," he informed Raider when he came back, "just like a hammer hits a nail."

"And hit it so hard," the other chopper added, "it'll go all the way through to China."

Then they climbed back up on the springboards and hacked into the cut with their axes. Raider and Silas waited.

At last the huge tree began to totter. There were a series of cracks—ten times louder than any pistol or rifle shots—and the huge mass began to go over. It sounded like a thunderclap an arm's length away. Then the continuing roar reminded Raider of a speeding train. The trunk hit the ground with a great thump, the shock of which traveled up their legs from the ground. The two choppers insisted that Raider search for the stake, although he readily admitted the trunk had driven it plumb through to China.

They went around the strips and warned the choppers to keep a wary eye out. After them, they warned the buckers, the men who sawed the redwood trunks into logs. But everyone had already been warned, and they clearly were not paying much heed, judging by the way Raider and Silas could approach most of them without any notice being taken of them. The way the men were spread out in pairs or small teams over a large area made it impossible to secure. They saw no signs of anybody on guard—everyone was working—in spite of what the bull buckers had told them.

"These independent-minded cusses ain't gonna listen to what I or anyone else tells them," Raider concluded. "Only way you and I can save their asses is to get to Stanton before he gets to them."

"Yeah, but where is he?"

"How the hell do I know? He could be over there behind that bush."

Stanton was not behind that bush. He was behind another, about half a mile away. He had kept one man with him and given the other two their orders. His plan was simple. They would operate in pairs against pairs of choppers and buckers. All they had to do was shoot, move, shoot, move, and shoot again. When the loggers panicked, they would head for the protection of their camp. Once in the camp, they would refuse to come out to work again so long as there were guns loose in the woods. No way could the Pinkertons flush them out of this forest. Stanton and his men could pin the loggers down in the camp as long as he pleased. Soon enough Cal Blair would have to say "No work, no pay." That was when the men would troop out wholesale to find work at other camps. The Eagle's cutting operations would be finished. Cal Blair would have to sell the sawmill.

If things went wrong, Stanton had a way out. He could travel due north to the big cuttings inland from Mendocino City, or even farther north to those in from

Fort Bragg, and hit the coast there. He was not expecting to need an escape route, but he had one just in case.

The loggers worked twelve hours a day. He had decided to wait until late afternoon before starting the shooting spree. He and his partner had selected several pairs of victims and planned how they would move from one set to the other with no loss of time once the shooting started. Surprise and shock would help them. Things would be easy at the beginning, so they needed to pack in as many hits as they could then.

Stanton cursed when he heard shooting. It was way too early for them to start. He didn't want too many hours of daylight left. Toward dusk the loggers would go to the camp and never come back out to work. This early, they might stand their ground and fight.

Shots sounded in fusillades. The choppers Stanton and his pard had been watching by now had dropped their axes and taken cover with their rifles. Stanton signaled his pard to stay down and wait. The other two men knew where to find them. In a couple of minutes, Stanton heard a man crashing headlong through the brush, coming in their direction.

The man came rushing up to them, giving their location away to the two choppers. "Stanton," he gasped, "it's the Pinkerton! He's here. The big one. The one called Raider."

Raider and Silas Hanks were continuing their tour when they heard yells and saw men running through the trees some distance ahead. One man whirled about, raised his rifle to his shoulder, and in quick succession shot three men following him. While Silas was saying, "That's one of Stanton's boys," Raider levered a shell

and raised his carbine to his shoulder. He picked off the
rifleman with a single shot.

One man kept running through the trees, looking behind him from time to time. He saw Raider, and Raider
remembered last seeing him soaking wet from the sinking of Stanton's boat. Because of the tree trunks, it was
hopeless trying to get a shot at him, and Raider didn't
waste his time.

The one Raider hit was dead, shot through the rib
cage. Two of the loggers were dead, and the third had a
shoulder wound and might live if they got him to Mendocino City for medical attention in time. Four loggers
carried him to camp, and more said they would help
bring him to the coast.

More loggers kept showing up all the time, coming
to investigate the shots. Raider had already set off on a
loping run after Stanton's man, with Silas Hanks puffing
along behind him.

With his hiding place given away by the hired gun
rushing up to him with the news that Raider was here,
Stanton opened fire on the two choppers they had been
watching. The choppers had taken cover with their
rifles, but Stanton nailed one of them who was not prop-
erly concealed. The man dropped his rifle, clutched at
his chest, and rolled on the ground, shouting to the
other chopper to help him.

His friend could not resist. Laying his rifle to one
side, he made a quick dart out from behind a tree trunk,
caught his fallen comrade by the armpits, and started to
drag him toward cover.

This was exactly what Stanton wanted. He had a
fresh cartridge levered into the chamber, and he had the

bead at the barrel's tip centered in the notch of the near sight. As soon as the second chopper showed, Stanton took his own sweet time in putting the bead at the center of his chest. His finger only stroked the trigger.

The logger stiffened, lost his hat, then pitched forward on top of the man he had been dragging. Stanton gave this wounded man a bullet in the neck to make sure of him.

He waved to his two hired guns to follow him, and all three men ran quickly to higher ground, to give them an advantage over anyone who came. They concealed themselves in a thick tangle of evergreen branches.

"Don't shoot unless they spot us," Stanton hissed. This was not how he had planned to do things, but all might yet turn out for the best. He had lost one man, but the loggers had lost five. Those men would think twice before leaving the camp for work the next day. There would be some foolhardy sorts who would insist. After he picked off one or two of them, there would be no more cutting while he stayed free in these woods. Right now, all he and his two men needed to do was to hide out until everyone had given up on them for today. The only fly in the ointment might be that damn Pinkerton.

Raider, Silas, and some loggers found the two choppers' bodies. Their tools were scattered at the base of the redwood they had been felling. Raider and the others walked around, looking for signs of where Stanton's man could have got to—they thought they were still dealing with a single fleeing man who had managed to shoot these two choppers as well as the previous three. The litter on the forest floor prevented any footprints from showing. Nothing showed where the fugitive had gone, and he could have traveled in almost any direction and soon been lost in the innumerable tree trunks.

Raider was tenacious. He refused to give up and carry the bodies back to camp. If he had to, he told the others, he would stay here till nightfall, and maybe beyond, looking for some sign to show itself. The loggers got restless after an hour or so, but they, along with others who had arrived, stuck it out, poking around to pass the time. Another hour passed before one man yelled, pointed, and threw himself on the ground.

All that time they had been in clear shooting view of not one but three riflemen in the tangle of bedding laid down for the redwood's fall. Bullets now sprayed out at them—but too late, everyone being jumpy enough to heed the warning and dive for cover.

In turn they now pinned down the three riflemen. They couldn't hit them, but they could prevent them from moving out before darkness fell.

Raider said urgently to Silas, "How much more work on that tree?"

Light dawned in Silas's eyes. "Maybe an hour with two men. No more than thirty minutes with all of us."

They provided cover as men ran to the huge tree. The cut was on the far side of the tree from the Stanton riflemen—Raider couldn't be sure Stanton himself was here—so the trunk protected them from hostile fire. Two men chopped like maniacs for as long as they could, then passed the axes to another two, who repeated the process. Six men between them got the first crack in less than ten minutes and toppled the tree in another fifteen minutes.

A hail of fire kept the gunmen down so the redwood could do its work.

It was another two days before the buckers sawed through the trunk in two places and an ox team dragged the log off the three bodies. One side of Stanton's face was still recognizable.

CHAPTER ELEVEN

While Cal Blair was pleased at the news that Stanton would no longer be a thorn in his side, news of another sort, brought to him by his bookkeeper, Ted Malloy, did nothing to raise his spirits. The six big steam-driven saws and log splitters destroyed by dynamite in Stanton's raid would cost more cash to replace than his company possessed. He needed these machines to stay in business. The saws and splitters remaining were being worked to capacity and couldn't handle the load. Malloy had facts and figures to back up everything he said. Cal rode into Mendocino City. The banks there were none too anxious to lend money to a company that was having his kind of problems.

"I can't say I blame them," Cal said.

"Borrowing might be the worst thing you could do right now," Raider opined. "It'd be one quick and sure-fire way for you to lose your company."

"He's right, Cal," Malloy said. "Jeff Dench could buy your credit notes from the banks, make you miss some repayment deadlines, and seize the company. That would be just one way he could go about doing it. And there's twenty other ways. Why don't you sell unmilled lumber to raise capital?"

The idea of selling redwood logs not cut into boards went against Cal Blair's inclinations, and the bookkeeper and his boss had a long argument about it. In the end, Malloy won when he pointed out for the fiftieth time that Cal had nothing else to sell except the mill itself and timber rights.

Next morning Cal took a schooner down to San Francisco, and the mill workers began putting a raft of logs together in the holding pond. Four days later Cal returned in a much more cheerful frame of mind. He had sold the uncut lumber to a sawmill on San Francisco Bay for a good price and had ordered replacement steam-operated saws and splitters.

A few days later the log boom of the holding pond was opened and a long cable was run out from the log raft inside the pond to the stern of a schooner anchored offshore. The schooner put up its sails and raised anchor. The ship appeared to be under full sail yet staying in one place for quite a while—like a ship in a bottle—until it advanced at a snail's pace toward the open sea and the huge raft of logs at the end of the cable eased slowly out of the holding pond. It took a long time for the raft to get clear of the rocks. The schooner kept heading for the open sea, its captain wanting his hard-to-handle burden to be far from this dangerous coast before he pointed his ship south.

The raft was nearly eight hundred feet long. The redwood logs were bound to one another with chains, and these chains alone weighed 175 tons. The logs would yield more than five million board-feet. The raft's fifty-foot beam, thirty-foot draft, and its big hogback many feet out of the water made it much larger than the biggest dead whale that might be found floating on the surface.

Passing schooners came close enough for their captains to use a spyglass to check who was hauling what. These seafarers kept close watch on one another. Even the most heavily loaded vessels passed the raft relatively fast. Weather was the captain's chief worry. In moderately rough seas, he might be forced to cut the raft loose and look for it again in calmer weather. Very rough water could break the raft and result in its total loss. However, the seas were calm, and the sky looked good for continuing fair weather.

The first two days passed uneventfully. In the early morning hours of the second night at sea, the man on watch saw the Point Arena lighthouse earlier than he expected to. A while later, he noted that the ship was making more progress southward in relation to the light than it should. Only then did the truth occur to him— the schooner was no longer being restrained by its heavy tow. He rushed to the stern and found the cable slack, then roused the captain from his sleep.

There was no panic. It was nothing for a cable to snap. They lowered the sails and hove to, intending to sail back at first light and reattach the cable to the raft. A log raft that size could not go far under its own power in calm water. Next morning the seas were still calm, but there was no sign of the raft.

Since an object as big as this log raft would be hard

not to locate at sea, the captain was not duly alarmed. Only after he had quartered a large area with his vessel did he suspect that something was wrong. He spent most of the day searching every possible place the raft could have drifted to, hailing passing vessels to ask if they had sighted it. Only when the sun began to drop in the western sky did he sail north, back to Little River, with the bad news.

Raider wanted to strangle the captain, refusing to believe that an object as large as that log raft could be lost by anybody under any conditions. He refused to go aboard and sail south with this captain, insisting that Cal Blair get rid of him and his crew. When Raider heard that Midnight Olsen's schooner had arrived in Mendocino City for loading, he rode in and persuaded the captain to sail south with him in search of the raft. Cal Blair made it worth the seaman's while with the offer of a generous reward.

Taking Samuel Trotter with him this time, Raider warned Cal and Silas Hanks to stick by the sawmill in his absence. There was no way of knowing if Jeff Dench had already found himself a replacement for Stanton, someone to start making trouble again in Little River. Certainly the disappearance of the raft hinted that Dench had found someone to continue his dirty work.

Midnight Olsen searched the area by daylight and ran close to the coastal coves—including those near Manchester—without locating the raft. The captain hailed passing ships without anyone being certain that they had seen the raft, though four rafts in progress south were reported to them by a number of vessels. Olsen's schooner caught up with all four rafts, only one of which was a hundred percent redwood. Both Raider and Trotter knew what the Little River raft looked like, and this all-redwood one was nothing like it in shape or size.

Olsen took his schooner to the farthest point south a raft the size of Cal Blair's could have been towed. By sundown, he gave up. He said to Raider, "I'd believe we missed it, lying lower in the water than it started because maybe the logs shifted, only that no one else has seen it. There's a lot of ships up and down this coast both by night and by day. By night, no one would see it unless he hit it and maybe be sunk by it. But by day, it's hard to believe it ain't been sighted if it's in these waters."

"All those men you been talking with can't be lying to you," Raider said. "If they ain't seen that raft all day, it's not here. The raft can't be onshore because we've run down all the way and looked for it. To me, that leaves only one other place—out to sea."

Midnight Olsen shook his head. "Impossible. You think they hitched a half-dozen schooners to the raft and towed it out of sight before the sun came up?"

"Or one steamboat," Trotter suggested.

Olsen flinched like he was stung. He gave Trotter a dirty look, like he had said a cussword in church.

Raider was interested. "That'd sure haul the wood out of sight quick enough. They say them steamboats is like the trains taking over from covered wagons. What do you say, Olsen?"

"They're not real seafarers," the captain said. "That's not real seamanship. No man's a true sailor unless he goes under sail."

"Damn it, Midnight, I couldn't give a shit about real seamanship," Raider said exasperatedly. "All I want to know is could a steamboat have taken that raft out to sea to wait for us to give up."

Olsen's hate of steam-powered vessels was too strong for him to concede this point. All he would say was, "At first light we'll head west and look for smoke-stacks."

After he had stomped away across the deck, Raider looked at Trotter curiously and said, "You know, it would never have occurred to me to think about newfan-gled gadgetry like a steamboat. I'm glad I brought you along, Trotter."

Trotter was grateful for the sunset and dusk, which hid his blush at this compliment. His most ambitious hope had been to avoid Raider's curses.

The sun was high next day before they sighted a steamer about forty miles off the coast.

"'Ceptin' we got this clear visibility and flat calm, we'd be looking for needles in a haystack," Midnight Olsen announced as he trained his spyglass on the steamer. "Goddamn dirty things send up so much smoke, it's a shame to let them on the water—although it sure makes them easy to spot."

"Is she towing anything?" Raider asked, bored by now with the sailing captain's constant denunciations of steam-powered vessels.

"Looks like it might be logs," Olsen said dryly, "though I can't say that I see Cal Blair's initials on them."

"You can leave that part to me," Raider said.

"See what the son of a bitch is doing?" Olsen said. "Heading south well beyond the shipping lanes. I'd swear this is our boy, Raider, unless he's pulling a big fishing net. He knows no lumber people ain't going to be out this far to catch him."

"He wasn't counting on Pinkertons," Raider said. "Right, Trotter?"

"It's logs all right," Olsen announced. "I'll bring you boys in for a close look at them and then you tell me what you want."

Both Raider and Trotter recognized the raft they had spent days watching as it was being put together at the holding pond in Little River.

"You want to board her?" Olsen asked.

"Sure. How do we do that? Fire a shot across her bow?" Raider asked, unwrapping his carbine from the oily cloth in which he had put it to protect it from sea-water and salt air.

"If her captain wants to make a break for it," Olsen answered, "all he has to do is cut the cable and head upwind. He can steam against the wind, while I have to tack. I couldn't catch him. But so long as that cable is attached, we can sail alongside him and you can jump aboard. If you want to take that chance."

Raider rewrapped the carbine and put it away. "You ready, Trotter?" he asked. "You may have to jump."

Trotter was more concerned over what kind of slaughter Raider might have in mind than over the dangers of leaping from one vessel to another. "I think you should handle this officially, Raider."

Raider grinned. "Show me how it's done, kid. You do the talking."

The seamen aboard the small steamboat waved to them and hollered in a friendly way. They got less friendly when the schooner came alongside. They offered no helping hand as the two men jumped from one pitching deck to the other.

"After you, sir," Raider said to Trotter.

Trotter approached the most authoritative-looking individual aboard, who had just come down an iron ladderway from the ship's bridge.

"Gentlemen, we are operatives of the Pinkerton National Detective Agency, and we have come aboard your vessel to seize property belonging to the Eagle Timber Company, which goods you are in illegal possession of. We call upon you to surrender these goods immediately or be answerable to us for your actions."

These words were hardly out of Trotter's mouth when a bullet whizzed past his ear. It came from Raider's gun, behind his back, and struck a crewman who had suddenly emerged from a cabin doorway with a shotgun leveled and ready to fire. The bullet hit the sailor in the gut, and his shotgun discharged as he fell to his knees, ripping a hole in the deck planks.

"As I said," Trotter continued in a calm voice, "we intend to repossess this property and will hold you and your men answerable for your actions."

The steamboat captain gaped from his dead crewmen to the fast-draw artist behind the little Pinkerton talking to him.

"I don't own them logs," he said. "I don't even own this boat."

"Who does?" Trotter asked sharply.

The man smirked. "I ain't saying."

"Put him over the side," Raider suggested to Trotter.

The captain looked once more at the rough-looking hombre with big mustaches and a leather jacket, with a still-smoking six-gun in his hand. He said, "This craft is registered to the Bay Navigation Company. Fella named Jeff Dench owns it. He's a builder down in San Francisco and has a sawmill at Manchester. I've never laid eyes on him, but like everyone else, I know him by name."

"How did you come by this raft?" Trotter asked.

The man paused before replying, took another look at Raider, and began to answer in a hurry. "Some lads in small sailboats had word the raft was on her way. They lay in wait and boarded her in darkness. They cut the line from the schooner. The wheelman must have been half asleep on the schooner—anyway they just sailed on. They signaled to us with lights. We secured a cable to the raft and had it twelve miles out to sea before day broke."

"What were you going to do with the raft?" Trotter asked.

"Follow orders. So far as I know, I was to bring it in to the Manchester sawmill when I got the word. I thought at first your schooner was bringing some of Dench's men, until I saw you was strangers."

"Idle the engine," Raider ordered. "Bring all your crew up on deck."

The captain did some yelling down hatchways, and, one by one, three men came out on deck. Raider searched them all at gunpoint and took two revolvers from them. He found a cartridge in the dead crewman's pocket and loaded it in the single-barrel shotgun, which he handed to Trotter. "Huddle all four of them over there," Raider told Trotter, confusing the captain, who had been assuming that Trotter was the one issuing instructions. "If they give you any reason, you'd do me a real favor by smearing them all against that cabin wall. I'm going below deck."

He walked around in the rusty passageways, dimly lit by oil lamps, looking into each cabin and space, gun ready. In one cabin doorway, he came face to face with a bearded man. All Raider could see for sure were the whites of his eyes and the gleam of an oil lamp on the revolver in his left hand. Raider squeezed the trigger of the Remington and the gun spat flame in the semidarkness. The man coughed once and slumped, his revolver rattling across the steel plates of the floor. When Raider collected this gun and had carefully checked out everyplace else, including the engine room, he climbed up on deck again. He made no comment about the gunshot they had all heard. Trotter knew better than to ask, and the seamen didn't have to.

"Who's the engineer?" Raider asked. One man stepped forward. "Who shovels coal?" When no one volunteered, Raider pointed to the huskiest crewman and said, "You'll do. Both of you go below and get that engine fired up. Try anything and I'll stuff the pair of you headfirst into the boiler."

The two crewmen headed for a hatchway fast, obviously believing they were escaping the execution the captain and other crewmen would suffer. Raider had them untie the cable from the steamboat's stern and toss it to the schooner. Meanwhile the idling steamboat was bumping alongside the redwood raft.

"Jump," Raider said, pointing over the side to the raft.

The men didn't take too long to brood about it.

The schooner was within shouting distance, and Raider called to Midnight Olsen. "As soon as we pull clear, take the raft down to San Francisco. You can feed and water these two critters so long as they don't cause you trouble. If they mess with the tow cable, let them die. Down in San Francisco, set them free."

"I hear you," Olsen confirmed.

"Take the wheel," Raider ordered Trotter. "Order full steam ahead."

"Me? Raider, I've never—"

"Trotter, this steamboat was your idea. Make it move!"

CHAPTER TWELVE

"Ain't no business of yours where we're going," Raider yelled down the hatchway. "Shovel coal, you bastard, or I'll come down and plug you."

As it happened, the men below were not the only ones who were concerned. Trotter, at the wheel, was beginning to be uneasy as the coast loomed up and Raider insisted on keeping a full head of steam. They had been under way a full five hours, during which the steamboat had been kept at top speed—a bit faster than a man's brisk walk on land. It was late afternoon as the steamboat neared the shore.

"I'll go up front and look out for rocks," Raider kindly offered. "It ain't so bad around here as up at Little River."

The coast had more sandy beaches in the Manchester region, but Trotter could see plenty of jagged rocks. He was no swimmer and took a less carefree attitude to such matters as personal safety than his Pinkerton colleague. Yet he dared not shout down to the engineer to reduce speed. Raider apparently was intent on some awful act of self-destruction, which would consume both him and Trotter, too. As Trotter saw it, there was nothing for him to do but die bravely and uncomplainingly. If he survived this, he swore to God, he would never ask to work with any legendary Pinkertons again. One thing Trotter felt sure of, he was never going to live long enough to become any kind of legend himself. He could see his end coming right before his eyes at this very moment, as the steamboat charged at the rocky coastline with the big loco gunfighter in the prow, waving to right or to left. Trotter spun the wheel as fast as he could and hoped for the best.

There were some ominous bangs and scrapes against the steel hull of the boat, which panicked the two men below decks. Raider called them up and stood them in the stern in case they'd be tempted to lower the head of steam and slow the boat. Trotter's eyes grew round when he realized that, with them on deck, there was no way to slow the boat. He could steer it, but that was all. He heard Raider yelling to them from the prow, couldn't understand what he wanted, then felt a sickening heave as the steamboat hit a mudbank.

The speed at which the boat was traveling caused it to plow through. Now they were in shallow water next to a holding pond full of logs. A sawmill was built on landfill next to the water and extended out over the water on redwood stilts.

Raider came running back and pulled the wheel from Trotter's hands. He headed the prow toward the sawmill. "Now's the time to jump, you lily-livered varmints!"

Jeff Dench was directing some men to unload a wagon of kerosene barrels at a distance from the sawmill. He was on a bluff above the mill and had a clear view out to sea.

"Don't bring those kerosene barrels any closer than this," he was saying. "You can come up here and get one when you need it. I shouldn't have to tell you this." He looked out at the steamer again. "Why are they coming in like that? This ain't San Francisco Bay. They'll run aground in another minute."

Dench only wished he could say what was really on his mind? What the hell was going on? Everybody he hired turned out to be an incompetent fool. After weeks of bungling, Stanton had finally managed to get himself killed. These idiots would have happily delivered a wagonload of kerosene into his sawmill if he hadn't been there. And now the steamboat that was supposed to be towing the raft at sea was coming into the rocky shallows at full speed with no raft in tow. Dench guessed they had either run out of coal or some misfortune had dispossessed them of the raft. So long as Cal Blair didn't get his hands on it again, things would still work out all right—though Dench had no wish to lose that fortune in redwood.

Then he saw something was really wrong. That steamboat was coming on like a herd of buffalo—straight at his sawmill. He cursed and half ran and half slid down a winding path on the bluff face, trying to reach his mill.

* * *

Raider spun the ship's wheel, aiming for the corner stilt supporting the sawmill extension over the water. He missed the stilt with the boat prow, and the steamer continued under the building. The clearance between the deck and floor of the mill was only a couple of feet. The sidewall of the mill crashed against the steel superstructure of the steamboat, shattering the plank wall. The impact was strong enough to twist the boat sideways— along with Raider's wild wheel twisting—and she heaved against three stilts, tearing them loose from the base of the building, bending them sideways on the boat deck with a huge crash.

Its weight drove the boat down in the water, and the boat's buoyancy in turn forced the building upward. The entire structure kept bouncing up and down in this way, breaking off or loosening other stilts, so that the entire part of the sawmill projecting out over the water was reliant on the steamboat wedged beneath it for support.

The impact of the steamboat's bridge against the side wall of the mill threw Samuel Trotter against a steel bulkhead and knocked him unconscious. Raider was flung against the ship's wheel and took some chest bruises and scratched ribs but stayed on his feet. The body of the seaman Raider had shot hours before was thrown into a grotesque sitting position. His eyes and mouth were open, and one stiff arm was extended, as if he were about to say something but had paused, not remembering what it was.

The engineer and crewman in the stern had clung to a rail and fallen forward onto coils of rope. Raider drew his revolver and threatened them.

"I told you swine to jump," his voice grated.

"The water is too deep," the engineer whined.

"Then get below and put the engine in reverse. Both of you. And don't try nothing so long as I'm up here breathing air with this gun in my hand."

Raider had a gift for communicating directly with people in emergencies. The two men rushed through a hatchway to do his bidding.

Raider poked Trotter in the side with his boot toe. "Come on, kid. Time to get moving."

To the millworker's fright, part of the mill floor suddenly dropped two to three feet and then began heaving up and down.

"Earthquake! Earthquake!" the men shouted, abandoning the saws and log splitters and running for the exits.

No one was hurt, which was lucky considering the big circular sawblades they were using to cut the wood. In their rush to escape, they left the machines running. They met their boss running toward them as they streamed out of the mill. They shouted at him, and he shouted at them, neither side making sense of what the other was saying. The sawmill had no windows, and they hadn't seen what Dench had seen. They had felt an earthquake and knew about the dangers of aftershocks. They refused to go back inside the building and tried to persuade Dench not to.

"Fuck the earthquake," Dench yelled. "That was my steamboat!"

This made no sense to the men, who stood at the front of the building on landfill and could not see from where they were the part that extended over water. When Dench waved a .45 Peacemaker in their faces, they backed off and let him risk his neck. None was foolhardy enough or felt enough loyalty to follow him.

Dench ran through the mill floor and jumped down on the pitching floor of the extension. Some of the steam-driven machines had stopped of their own accord, while others ran on by themselves. The pitching up and down had dislodged enough planks from the side wall to show clearly the ship's bridge against it.

A brilliant idea occurred to Dench. By now he had realized that the Pinkertons had seized control of the raft and this steamboat. He would enter by way of the captain's bridge—an entrance he was entitled to—come down the gangway, and surprise the Pinkertons. No one could hold it against him for blasting the pair of them in cold blood as they destroyed his property.

He dragged a ladder and set it up against the disintegrating mill wall. After leaning the ladder top against the ship's bridge, he placed a block of wood at the ladder base to keep it from slipping. Then, Peacemaker in his right hand, he scrambled quickly up the rungs.

This chanced to be the very moment when the engineer had built up another head of steam and put the ship's engine in reverse. The steamboat jerked and scraped its way backward out from under the building.

Raider heard the shout and saw, through falling wall boards, Dench's ladder topple. Dench fell on his side on a heavy trestle table. The fall stunned him, and for the moment he was not sure where he was or what was happening to him. He felt himself being dragged over the table surface, and a high-pitched whine sang in his ears.

The Pinkerton, hardened as he was to all kinds of sights, looked away as the cables drew Dench horribly screaming into the spinning circular sawblade. Then the screaming stopped, and when Raider looked again, only Dench's legs and lower torso were still on the table, to one side of the scarlet-stained sawblade.

But now the steamboat was free in the water, and the sawmill extension plunged with a great splash into the drink. The machines chattered inside, and great billows of steam rose as hot pipes hit cold seawater.

The two horses hitched to the wagon on the bluff over the mill were spooked by the noise and spectacular collapse. They bolted, breaking a wagon shaft and ripping out of their harness. The wagon tipped over, and its load of barrels came rolling down the steep bluff. The millworkers saw them coming and ran for their lives.

Barrel after barrel tumbled down and smashed into staves and hoops against the side of the sawmill situated on landfill. One rolling metal barrel hoop sparked on a stone, and the spilled kerosene went up in a huge blaze against the plank wall of the mill.

Meanwhile the steamboat was moving aimlessly backward, hitting against the log boom of the holding pond, as Raider cursed and spun the ship's wheel. He didn't want the engine in forward again in case it would bring him back toward the sawmill.

Knowing he just couldn't get the hang of this contraption, Raider booted Trotter in the side once more. "Let's go, sonny boy. We have work to do."

Ever obedient, Samuel Trotter staggered to his feet and shook his head to clear it. The last he remembered, Raider was steering the steamboat at the sawmill. Now Trotter saw part of the mill half submerged in seawater and the rest of it blazing in huge sheets of flame.

"My God, Raider, what have you done?"

Raider only cackled in satisfaction.

Trotter was looking very serious. "How can I explain this in my report to headquarters?"

Raider snorted. "Easy, kid. Just tell them you was with me."